THE WOMAN IN THE EMERALD DRESS

A LAKE MURRAY MURDER MYSTERY

BOOK 3

STEVEN JACOBS

OTHER WORKS BY THE AUTHOR

ALSO BY STEVEN JACOBS

THE WOMAN IN THE EMERALD DRESS

DRESS

A LAKE MURRAY BOOK

By: Steven Jacobs

The *butterfly effect* is a concept from the chaos theory widely used to describe situations where seemingly minor actions can have drastic consequences elsewhere.

To my Family and friends who have supported me in putting my stories down on paper.
For Carly, without your love and support, this book would not have been possible.

"I'm not working on The Great American Novel. All I'm doing, I hope, is entertaining readers."
Clive Cussler

PROLOGUE

Early 2024, Long Beach, California

Stefan and Cecilia Rhodes' driver pulled into the marina, where the three-hundred-foot yacht *Omertà* was docked. Following the directions on the envelope, the limousine driver pulled up to the boat slip, parked, and hurriedly walked to the back door to let Stefan and Cecilia out.

Stefan stared at his wife as they exited the back and smiled, "What?" Cecilia asked coyly.

Before answering, Stefan let his eyes wander, following the plunging neckline of her evening gown halfway down to her slim waist, and said, "Nothing, you simply look ravishing in that evening gown."

"You don't look so bad yourself," Cecilia said as she admired her husband in his perfectly fitted suit.

"Are you ready to go, my dear?" Stefan asked.

"Ready as I'll ever be," Cecilia replied, even though the face she made said otherwise.

"What is it?" Stefan asked.

"Nothing. I just don't like this. That's all," Cecilia replied. "Just what will you do if you get caught with your so-called insulin pump?" Cecilia asked as she air-quoted the insulin pump.

"I'm not going to get caught. These guards are just hired thugs. They don't have the proper training. We're just here to rub elbows with the big boys, have a good dinner, and that's all."

"Yes, I know, but you know who owns this yacht we're about to go out on," Cecilia said, "and what do you hope to gain from this?"

"There are rumors that it's owned by Lorenzo Sorrentino, but nothing has been confirmed, and there's nothing to say that he will be here tonight. Also ... one never knows when a recorder will come in handy."

"Yes, honey, but just being on a yacht associated with the Sorrentino syndicate would be bad for your company's image," Cecilia said as she tried to talk some sense into her husband one last time.

As they talked, yet another limousine pulled up, and both watched as more guests showed up for the exclusive dinner cruise. No sooner had the other guests got out of their stretched limousine than Cecilia's eyes widened and said softly, "Do you see who that is?"

"I see who it is," Stefan replied, speaking of Henri Sardou, a French national rumored to be one of Europe's best burglars and safe crackers.

"I wonder what he's doing here?" Cecilia asked.

"Nothing good. I assure you," Stefan said as they started to walk down the dock to the awaiting yacht, already bustling with guests and staff.

As they neared the line of guests waiting to go through security, Stefan leaned in and whispered in Cecilia's ear, "Look up ahead of us. Do you know who the redhead is?"

"No. Should I?" Cecilia asked, concerned as she looked at the middle-aged gentleman with striking red hair and a neatly cropped beard.

Stefan said, "No, but his name is Sebastian MacGowan, and he is the son of a big-time Irish mobster up in Philadelphia. Not only that, but my people have heard rumors that Henri Sardou has done work for the Irish."

Cecilia digested what Stefan said, then asked, "Does Sorrentino know this?"

"Nobody knows what Sorrentino does or doesn't know," Stefan replied, "which is another reason for the insulin pump."

They saw a small line of guests waiting to board as they approached the yacht. One by one, each couple gave their names to a staff member who checked them off a register. After that, each person emptied their pockets and was scanned with a hand-held metal detector, and the women's purses were searched before they were allowed onboard.

As Stefan was being searched with the hand wand by one of the guards, an audible beep emanated from one of Stefan's pockets. "What do you have? The guard asked. "You were supposed to empty your pockets."

Slowly, Stefan slid his hand into his pocket and produced a small device about the size of a pager. He showed it and the tube connecting it to a port on his side and said, "It's an insulin pump. I can't take it off. Sorry, I should have told you."

"No problem, sir," the guard replied as he finished handwanding Stefan.

Immediately upon being allowed to board, a staff member stood waiting to hand each person a glass of champagne as they crossed a small gangway. "It worked like a charm. Didn't it?" Stefan asked.

"Yes, but I still don't like this. Something tells me this is a terrible idea. You should not have brought that thing." Cecilia said, speaking of the hidden recorder.

Smiling, Stefan replied, "Lighten up and have a little fun, my darling. Everything will be fine. I assure you."

Cecilia rolled her eyes and said, "Yeah, I'm sure someone said that before the Titanic set sail for New York, too."

"Stop," Stefan playfully scolded his wife, "now go mingle until it's time to eat dinner."

"Well, there are a few other women I see that I know," Cecilia replied, "the night might not be a total loss. Just be careful, please."

Chuckling slightly, Stefan replied, "I will ... and you be careful too."

Cecilia smiled coyly and asked, "Why must I be careful? Don't you trust me?"

"Trust you, yes ... trust others on this yacht with my smokin' hot wife ... no."

Cecilia giggled and said, "I'll be fine. I'm just going to go mingle with the ladies."

Thirty minutes later, the dinner guests were treated to a delightful meal of grilled salmon, scallops, and shrimp, followed by a selection of delicious desserts.

As the night wore on, Cecilia noticed several members of the waitstaff kept coming and going through double doors closely guarded by two men who obviously had weapons discreetly hidden under their jackets.

"I wonder what's back there," Cecilia said as she watched several people come and go.

"I have no idea, and I'm not sure I want to know," Stefan replied, "those bulges under their jackets scream TEC-9s."

Just then, a man neither Stefan nor Cecilia knew walked up to their table and said, "Mr. Rhodes, will you follow me, please?"

Stefan and Cecilia exchanged glances at one another, and then he asked, "What's this about?"

"Someone just wants to have a conversation with you, that's all. Now, if you'll please leave your phone here and follow me," the man replied, the tone in his voice indicating that he was not asking.

As he stood up to follow the man, Stefan saw the look on Cecilia's face as if she were pleading with her eyes for Stefan not to go, "It will be all right. I won't be gone long," Stefan said reassuringly as she watched him push a button on his insulin pump. He bent down, gave his wife a peck on the cheek, pulled his phone out of his pocket, and left it with his wife.

The man who had walked up to the table snapped his fingers, and within moments, a member of the waitstaff appeared, "Yes, sir! What can I do?"

The unnamed man looked at the waiter and said, "Refresh the lady's drink, please."

Before Cecilia could protest, the waiter replied, "At once!" before tearing off to get another champagne glass.

Without another word, Stefan followed the unnamed man from the table to the double doors, where the two men stood guard. Cecilia watched as they approached the door as one of the guards opened it. She could briefly see inside the room, and what she saw sent a shiver into her soul.

When the door opened, Cecilia could see deep into the room. Even though the door was opened for just a few seconds, there was no doubt that she saw none other than Lorenzo Sorrentino, the boss of the Sorrentino crime syndicate.

As the door closed behind her husband, Stefan, the waiter returned with a fresh champagne glass and said, "Here you are, madam. Can I get you anything else?"

Cecilia paused momentarily, finding it hard to form a sentence as a huge lump formed in her throat from the sense of doom that came over her, "No—no, thank you. I'm fine."

"As you wish," the waiter said before walking off.

Twenty minutes later, the double doors that Stefan entered once again opened up. Stefan walked back over to the table where Cecilia was still seated. As soon as he sat down, Cecilia noticed Stefan was white as a sheet and asked, "What in the hell happened? Did I see Lorenzo Sorrentino back there?"

"Leave it alone," Stefan snapped.

"I will not leave it alone," Cecilia snapped sternly, "you need to tell me what's going on, and you need to tell me now."

"I can't," Stefan calmly replied.

"Can't or won't?" Cecilia asked.

Stefan took a deep breath, leaned in, put his elbows on the table, and said, "The less you know, the better it is, and that's all I can or will say for now, but I need you to do something." Without waiting for her to answer, Stefan leaned forward so the table was masking what he was doing, removed the recording device disguised as an insulin pump, and handed it to Cecilia under the table. "Put it in your purse."

"What? Why?" Cecilia asked, concerned.

"Just do it! Stefan said sharply under his breath, "If something happens—"

"What do you mean if something happens?" Cecilia asked softly.

Stefan took a deep breath, smiled, and said, "Honey, don't worry. Just put it in the bottom of your purse, and don't think about it again for the rest of the night."

Even though the overall mood onboard was jovial and festive, the tension at the Rhodes table was so thick it could be cut with a knife. Cecilia was quiet for a few minutes and then said quietly, "This is not over. We will finish this conversation at home. You may not believe it, but I have just as much to do with the business as you do."

"I know you do, honey. And I fully expect to have a conversation when we get home. There are just some things that we should not talk about right here. Now, other people are watching. Would you please at least try to have a good time?"

Cecilia casually looked around to see other couples glancing at the pair as they chatted about the goings-on in the back room. "It's hard to have a good time on a yacht owned by one of the biggest syndicates on the west coast!" Cecilia snapped a little louder than she thought.

Just then, the unknown man who had summoned Stefan to the back room approached the table and asked, "Is everything all right here?"

Stefan smiled and said, "Yes, everything is quite all right. My wife and I are simply having a ... discussion. Nothing more."

"Perhaps another glass of champagne would help?" The man asked.

"Yes, of course," Stefan replied.

The unknown man snapped his fingers, and within a few

moments, another waiter appeared, holding a tray with two fresh glasses of champagne for Stefan and Cecilia.

Cecilia took a glass, and then Stefan took the remaining glass. The waiter had scarcely left the area before Cecilia downed the glass of champagne in one gulp.

Within minutes of drinking the last glass of champagne, Cecilia slurred, saying, "I—I don't feel so good."

"It's no wonder you don't feel good. You've had three or four glasses of champagne tonight, along with a big meal and dessert."

Ignoring Stefan, Cecilia slurred, "I'm burning up. I want to go out on deck. Maybe ... maybe that will help a little."

Stefan, who was picking at the rest of his food, looked up at Cecilia and said, "Your cheeks are a bit red. Perhaps some fresh air would do you some good."

As Cecilia got up, Stefan stood and said, "Here, let me help you."

"I ... I can manage," Cecilia stuttered as she slowly got to her feet, grabbed her purse, and attempted to brush off Stefan's attempt to help her.

Stefan plopped back down in the chair and picked at his remaining food. Shortly, a waiter came around and asked if he would like an after-dinner coffee, which Stefan gladly accepted.

A few minutes later, the waiter returned and asked, "Will the lady be having a coffee as well?"

"Yes, please," Stefan replied.

Stefan sat in peace for a few minutes, casually looking around or making small talk as someone walked by. However, as the minutes ticked by, he became slightly unnerved when Cecelia didn't return.

Stefan got up and started walking toward the sliding door leading onto the large back deck. As he approached the door, it suddenly slid open as someone was returning from the deck. Stefan smiled, expecting to see his wife coming back in, but instead, he saw a man he knew as Marco Russo coming back in.

Marco was nicknamed "the hammer" because he was known to be the syndicate's fixer, chief muscleman, and Lorenzo Sorrentino's personal bodyguard.

Stefan immediately got a bad feeling in the pit of his stomach, "Did you see my wife outside?"

"How should I know who your wife is?" Marco scoffed before moving past Stefan and walking into the back room.

Stefan walked out on the empty deck, but Cecilia was nowhere to be found. After looking around for her for several minutes, Stefan became noticeably worried. Then, a crew member approached him, asking what was wrong.

After telling the crew member he could not find his wife and that she was last seen coming out on the deck, the crew member immediately radioed the captain to tell him they had an unaccounted-for guest. Within minutes, a search was launched for Stefan's wife, who was nowhere to be found.

WITHIN MINUTES of the onboard search turning up nothing, the ship's captain immediately ordered all exterior lighting to be turned on and all available crew topside to look for the missing woman.

The captain also reversed course to start a search for the missing woman and notified the Coast Guard as well. The festive mood of the dinner party slowly died away as word spread that a guest who had too much to drink possibly fell overboard.

After searching for the better part of the night, Cecilia Rhodes was not located, and the yacht was forced to return to shore because of a lack of fuel despite Stefan's pleas to keep looking. The Captain of the ship spoke with Stefan and assured him they had done all they could, and a helicopter from the US Coast Guard was already racing to the scene. On the return trip to Long Beach, Stefan mostly sat in stunned silence as the shock of what had happened set in.

After returning to the dock, members of the Coast Guard and local police detectives boarded the *Omertà*. They took brief statements from several guests and only stayed aboard for less than twenty minutes; detectives were satisfied that it seemed to be nothing more than a tragic accident. Detectives then escorted Stefan Rhodes home.

By the time Stefan got home, it was nearly six o'clock the following morning. Cecilia and Stefan's daughter, Emily, met Stefan at the door, wild-eyed and panicked. After breaking the news to Emily that her mother was gone, Emily broke down crying, collapsing into a heap on the front steps of their home, so much so that Stefan had to pick her up and carry her back into the house.

Coast Guard helicopters and several patrol boats searched the waters throughout the next few days. After an extensive search, Cecilia's body was never located, and eventually, the search was suspended indefinitely.

1

Several months later, Lake Murray, SC

While everyone boarded *The Spirit of Lake Murray*, an eighty-foot-long Skipperliner yacht specially renovated into a dinner cruise vessel for Lake Murray, chatter could be heard from most of the couples eager for an excellent meal and a beautiful moonlit cruise on the lake.

The Spirit of Lake Murray was the perfect venue for couples to have a romantic dinner for two, an anniversary celebration, or even a dinner party. It was a little out of the ordinary but not unheard of when a woman in an emerald dress was one of the last to board alone, holding what appeared to be a sketchpad for the sunset cruise.

As *The Spirit of Lake Murray* slowly pulled away from the dock and headed out into Lake Murray, most aboard, including the woman in a stunning emerald dress, walked onto the open-air upper deck to get an unobstructed view of the surrounding lake. Before long, everyone aboard had settled in, including the mysterious woman in the emerald dress who had staked out a spot near the rail with her sketchpad, apparently waiting for something that piqued her interest.

Finally, as the sun set on Lake Murray, passengers were treated to a spectacular show of dazzling shades of deep orange mixed in with the perfect array of clouds as the sun went down. As the sunset changed by the moment, many aboard took the opportunity to snap photos of the stunning sunset with their phones while the woman in the emerald dress sketched what she saw on her pad.

After the magic of the sunset dissipated, the partygoers' "oohs and ahhs" faded as they returned to their tables to prepare for the feast to come. As the woman in the emerald dress found a table and took a seat, she continued to work on her sketch, occasionally looking around as if she were looking for someone.

The woman sat at the table alone, working on her sketch, when a waitress approached her and asked if she wanted to order dinner. "Yes, but I'm not terribly hungry. I'm not sure what to order," the woman replied.

"Well then, might I suggest the Chicken Diablo Sandwich? It has an amazing house-made pepper aioli and pickle relish. It's to die for!" The waitress said.

"Sounds perfect," the woman replied, "I'll have that."

"Excellent choice," the waitress replied as she wrote the order down.

As the waitress turned to walk away, the woman in the emerald dress said, "Excuse me, I was supposed to be meeting someone onboard. Would you happen to know if another person is here alone tonight?"

"I am not sure, but I will be sure to keep my eye out for you," the waitress said with a wink and a sly smile, indicating she thought it was supposed to be a romantic encounter.

Shortly thereafter, the waitress returned with the woman's order, grinned, and said, "Now that I have a moment, I am going to walk up to the upper deck and see what I can see for you."

Before the woman could stop the waitress, she turned and walked off. Less than ten minutes later, the waitress returned and said, "I found someone on the upper deck, and he is definitely alone."

"Thank you. I can't see how I missed him," the woman in the emerald dress replied.

"Well, he's not going anywhere for at least another hour, so eat your dinner before it gets cold," the waitress replied, smiling.

The waitress walked off to help other patrons for a few minutes and let the woman in the emerald dress eat her meal in peace. After a bit, the waitress walked past, winked, and said, "He's still there, just so you know."

The woman smiled at the waitress, left her sketchbook at her table, and made her way through the other passengers to the upper deck near the yacht's stern, deciding to let the mystery man come to her.

Not long afterward, a heavy burning smell filled the area as concern spread among the passengers of *The Spirit of Lake Murray*. It was not long before black smoke could be seen hanging in the air. As the smell and the smoke worsened, panic started to spread throughout the passengers as they turned their attention from their conversations to the more pressing matter of a possible fire onboard.

Immediately, the crew sprang into action and located the source of the burning smell. As it turns out, a small fire started in the men's bathroom from an unknown source. Nobody at the time knew or realized the fact that the fire was set intentionally as a diversion.

In less than five tense minutes, the fire was quickly extinguished with no injuries other than the frayed nerves of some passengers.

As quickly as it had started, the situation was over. Captain Rick came around and assured everyone that the issue had been taken care of; however, out of an abundance of caution, he had decided to cut the cruise short and return to the dock to determine what, if any, damage had been done to the yacht's facilities.

ON THE UPPER OPEN-AIR DECK, the woman in the emerald dress stood at the stern of the yacht looking out across the lake, oblivious of what was happening on the lower deck when someone came up from behind her, placed a hand over her mouth, and hissed, "Did you really think we wouldn't find out? The syndicate sends its regards."

In one well-practiced movement, the mystery man pulled a knife expertly from under his belt and buried it between the woman's ribs, instantly taking her ability to fight or scream for help. When the mystery man felt the woman's body relax, he glanced over his shoulder to ensure nobody was watching.

Once he was sure everyone's focus was on the possible fire on the lower deck, he pushed the woman's body off the stern of the yacht and into the darkness of Lake Murray.

THE FOLLOWING DAY, Lexington County Sheriff Detectives Amy Stone and her partner Raylon "Big Nims" Cross were sitting in their shared cubicle, working on paperwork, when Raylon's phone started ringing.

In one well-practiced move, Raylon reached over and hit a button on his desk phone without ever taking his eyes off his computer screen, "Cross here," he said with his deep Alabama twang.

"You and Stone get your butts over to my office," Chief of Detectives Boone snapped.

Without missing a beat, Cross replied, "We're almost caught up with paperwork. We will have it for you by the end of our tour today, boss."

"That can wait," Boone snapped as Stone stopped what she was doing and began to listen, "You two have a new case. Now get over here."

Stone piped in and said, "We got the last case. Can't you give it to Peters or Williams instead?"

"You two have the lowest number of open cases, so the answer is no. You're taking this one. Now stop what you're doing and get to my office."

"Yes, boss," Cross said before hanging up.

Stone looked at Cross and said, "Come on, big man. Time to make our pay."

Both got up and walked through the maze of cubicles dubbed the bullpin and over to Chief of Detectives Stephen Boone's office.

When Stone knocked on the closed door, they heard, "Enter."

Stone opened the door, and she and Cross walked in and started to sit in the chairs in front of Boone's desk. "Don't bother to sit. You won't be here long enough. I just got notified that a body was found inside a residence in the ritzy Lakeside Plantation neighborhood off of Corley Mill Road."

As soon as Stone heard the name of the neighborhood, she rolled her eyes and said, "Oh, no ... it's going to be one of those kinds of cases. I can just feel it."

"And just what are we getting into?" Cross asked.

Stone replied, "Let's just say this: I've heard the homes in that neighborhood start at half a million."

"So, bougie people with more money than sense," Cross replied.

"Exactly," Stone said with a smile.

"Are you two going to sit here chatting about it all day? Get out of my office and see what the hell's going on," Boone prodded.

TWENTY MINUTES LATER, Stone and Cross turned off the winding Corley Mill Road and pulled into the fancy yet not overly extravagant Lakeside Plantation neighborhood where big houses and perfectly manicured lawns were the norm.

As they pulled into the neighborhood, Cross said, "Man! There are some huge homes in here."

Stone smiled and said, "Yeah, but as we know, there are much bigger and more extravagant homes on the lake."

"So, what you're saying is this is the trailer park for the upper class," Cross said as he gawked at the size of the homes.

"Yeah, essentially," Stone said, chuckling, "and I bet half of these homes have pools in the backyard, too."

"Probably ... back home in Alabama; if we wanted to cool off and go for a swim, we had to go down to the creek," Cross said with a smile as he reminisced about his childhood.

"In the creek?" Stone asked, shocked.

"Oh, yeah, the water was so black you couldn't see your hand under two inches of water. We had no idea if snakes were around, but we didn't care."

Stone shook her head, giggled, and said, "And you were worried about the lake?"

"Yeah, well, our creek wasn't two hundred feet deep either," Cross said with a chuckle.

As Stone turned the corner, they were confronted with what bystanders would consider a circus, but to the experienced detectives, it was controlled chaos.

Stone and Cross noticed they were on a short road ending in a cul-de-sac. At the end of the road, Lexington County Sheriff's deputies stretched crime scene tape across the street and barred everyone from entering except law enforcement.

Stone and Cross had to park across the cul-de-sac and walk to the crime scene house. A shiny black BMW 7 sat in the driveway as a status symbol on full display.

"Beautiful car," Stone said, admiring its shiny exterior and sleek lines as she walked past.

"Yeah, but considering why we're here, I'm betting he should have invested the money he spent on that car in a better security system," Cross replied.

As they approached the front door, Stone asked, "Who was the responding officer?"

"That would be me," the officer replied. "I'm Deputy Jones. I got the call for a wellness check at about 1300 hours. Housekeeping showed up to clean the house, but the single male occupant of the home, a man named Michael Hawkins, would not come to the door."

"And she was sure he would be here?" Cross asked.

"I asked the same question, and she told me that he had a standing reservation for cleaning at this time once a week. She said he had never missed his appointment, and she identified the black BMW in the driveway as his. When I arrived, she told me she knew he had a heart problem, and she was scared he could be having a medical emergency.

The front door is locked and solid as a bank vault, so I decided to check the rest of the house. As I went through the side gate, I noticed a lock on the ground that looked like it had been eaten with acid or something. I called and got permission to force entry into the house. Turns out, I didn't need to force entry because the back door was open."

"Open as in cracked or wide open?" Cross asked.

"No, I checked the handle, and the door was unlocked. I cracked the door open and announced myself but got no response, so I made entry into the home, and that's when I found the deceased. Somebody did a real number on him. I haven't seen that much blood at one crime scene in a long time."

"I want to see that lock," Stone said.

"Not a problem. Right this way," Jones said as he started to lead the two detectives around the corner of the home to the gate.

As they approached the gate, they saw the remnants of the lock on the ground. Stone and Cross knelt to examine the lock closer. "Looks like some kind of acid or something," Cross said.

"Sure does," Stone replied as she took her pen out and moved the remnants of the lock around on the ground. "Somebody came prepared," she said to no one in particular.

"Yeah, and wait until you see the inside," Deputy Jones said.

"Show us," Stone replied.

The deputy hesitantly said, "Okay, but just so you know ... it's bad."

Deputy Jones took the detectives into the dining room, and what they saw was unimaginable. The dining table and chairs had been pushed off to one side of the room, and a male figure was tied in a chair and sitting in the middle of the room, bloodied and beaten to a pulp.

"Jesus, look at this guy," Stone said, "someone really did a number on this poor guy."

"I'll say," Cross replied as he knelt to get a better look at the man who had obviously been dead for quite a while. To ensure his screams didn't attract attention, whoever did this shoved a dishrag from the kitchen in his mouth. Both of the man's eyes were swollen shut and bruised from multiple blows. His nose had obviously been broken, and his lip was split wide open.

Stone examined the room and said, "This took a lot of time. This was no murder ... this was torture."

"Agreed," Cross said, "either someone hated this guy and really wanted him to suffer, or he had information somebody needed."

"Exactly, and if whoever did this didn't know he had a heart condition, it's possible they didn't even mean to kill him. Do we know if there are security cameras or not?"

"There is a security system but no cameras," Jones replied.

"Okay, let's back out of here. We need to get a search warrant for the entire house and call the coroner if that hasn't been done already," Stone said. "In the meantime, I want to talk to the maid who called it in."

All three left the residence and went back outside to find the woman from housekeeping who called 911. Once back in front of the home, Deputy Jones pointed out the woman who called for the welfare check. Stone went to talk to her while Cross stepped away to place calls to the coroner and their boss to ensure they get a search warrant for the home.

As Stone walked up, she said, "Hello, I'm Detective Amy Stone with the Lexington County Sheriff's Office. Can you tell me your name, please?"

"Yes, of course," the older woman said, "it's Hattie Porter, with two t's."

"So, can you tell me what happened?"

"I already told the other officer, but sure, I'll tell you too, I suppose. Mr. Hawkins has a standing order to have his house cleaned once a week and never misses it. I showed up today, like always, and his car was in the driveway as usual, just like it should be.

Usually, I ring the doorbell, and he meets me at the door with a warm and friendly smile because that's the type of person he was, and he was a good tipper, too. Well, I rang the doorbell, and he never came to the door. After a while, I began to get worried because I knew he had a heart condition, so I called the police."

"Did you see anyone or anything out of the ordinary?" Stone asked.

"No. Everything is just as it should be except for the fact that he never came to the door. He was such a good man," Porter said as tears ran down her cheeks.

Stone asked, "By any chance, do you know what he did for a living?"

"Not exactly. I know it has something to do with buying and selling art. You know, the fancy art that people pay too much for."

Stone smiled and said, "Yeah, I get it. Did he have an office in the house?"

Mrs. Porter thought momentarily and said, "I'm not sure, but I can tell you there was a room downstairs off the hallway that was always locked. I've never seen the inside of that room, so I guess there could be an office in there."

"Okay, thank you for your help," Stone replied.

"You're welcome. I just wished I could have done more," Porter replied, wiping the tears from her eyes.

"Mrs. Porter, can we call someone to drive you, or will you be all right?"

"I'll be fine. Besides, I have to get to my next appointment."

"Okay, but I need to remind you that this is an ongoing investigation, and you can't talk about what's happening here."

"How am I going to say anything? I don't know anything," Porter said, sniffling and wiping tears off her cheek.

Stone put her arm around her and gently ushered her toward her car, "Officer Jones, will you see to it that Mrs. Porter gets out of the area, okay?"

"Yes, ma'am," Jones replied. He then helped her into her car and guided her away from the area.

As Mrs. Porter pulled away, Cross said, "How is the maid doing?"

"She's upset, and rightfully so, but she'll be okay."

"Did she see anything?" Cross asked.

"No, which is good. She would have never been the same if she had actually gone inside. Anyway, where are we?"

"Dr. Singh at the coroner's office is already on the way, and I called Boone. The digital warrant should be on your phone shortly, and he has already given the green light to go ahead and start searching."

Before Stone could even respond, her phone dinged. With just a few taps on her smartphone, Stone smiled and said, "And there's the digital warrant. Let's go."

2

S tone and Cross went back into the house, foregoing the room where the body was and focusing on the rest of the house. Walking through the rest of the house, they were struck by how pristine it was.

After a brief walkthrough of the kitchen, it became clear that nothing was out of place. The kitchen looked like a photo from Better Homes and Garden magazine. The living room was still full of high-end electronics, from a Samsung eighty-five-inch television hanging on the wall to a state-of-the-art surround system.

There were also numerous valuable antiques and artwork worth tens of thousands of dollars hanging on the walls. "Well, we know this wasn't a burglary," Stone said.

"Yeah, or this entire place would have been cleaned out," Cross replied, "especially if this happened last night because they would have had time to clean the whole house out."

"Which is why there is much more here than meets the eye," Stone replied.

"Agreed," Cross said, "I'll be very interested in seeing what's behind the locked door the maid told you about."

"So will I," Stone replied, "let's find out."

As Stone and Cross walked down the hallway, they came to a door that had been kicked in. "I'd say this was the room the maid was talking about," Cross said as he examined the door."

"Yeah, I'd say you're right. There's a footprint here on the door by the handle, but by the looks of it, it's going to be a work boot or military type of boot. We can probably get a size from it, but that will be about it."

"That's better than nothing," Cross replied as he cautiously stepped into the room that was once locked. Cross said as they looked around, "Looks like this was an office."

"Yeah, but it's been ransacked now," Stone said as she walked around to the back of the desk to find all the drawers had been pulled out and the contents strewn about on the floor.

As they carefully looked around without disturbing too much before a crime scene photographer got there, Stone said, "This looks like an ordinary home office to me. Nothing here would suggest something to warrant something like what happened in the dining room."

Cross, examining a set of built-in bookshelves behind the desk, said, "Yeah, but there has to be something. Whoever did this took their time, which meant one of two things. They either wanted to torture the guy for the pure enjoyment of it, or they were after something he knew or had."

Stone considered what Cross had said and replied, "Let's hope it's the latter. I'd hate to think someone is running around our town who could do this to another human being for the enjoyment of it."

After carefully searching the papers strewn around on the floor, Cross said, "Ya know, I have to agree with you. I'm not seeing anything here either."

Stone stopped what she was doing, turned to face Cross, and said, "Which leads us back to our human punching bag in the other room. The question goes back to why."

Cross thought momentarily and said, "Whoever did this ransacked this particular room looking for something. The question is, what was it, and did they find it?"

"There's another question we need to find out also," Stone said.

"Which is what?"

Stone said, "As we have both noticed, this so-called office has nothing to do with his job of being in the art world. With that being said, he's gotta have another office somewhere. So, where is it, and did whoever beat this man to death get the answer out of him before he died?"

"That is an excellent question," Cross replied, suggesting he was unsure what to do next. "Well, if there's nothing here for us, and time is not on our side, let's go back to the office and do a public records search and see if he has any property at another location. We can't do much more here until the entire crime scene is photographed anyway."

"Sounds like a plan," Stone said as they left the room, leaving everything exactly as they found it.

As the pair retraced their steps into the hallway and back towards the front of the home, they heard a distinctly familiar voice coming from the dining room where the body was located. As Stone and Cross approached, a sudden bright blue flash bounced off the walls as the crime scene photographer began his work.

Stone and Cross stopped in the doorway, peering in to see none other than Dr. Sandeep Singh, Lexington County's Coroner, and several of his team beginning their work. Stone said, "Dr. Singh, I know you just got here, but can you tell me how long he's been dead?"

Without looking up at Stone, Singh said with his distinctly Indian accent, "I cannot tell you how he died yet, but I can safely say he died between ten o'clock last night and two o'clock this morning; anything else would be a guess at this point. I won't know more until I get the victim back to the morgue."

"Thank you, Dr. Singh. Also, the maid who called it in said she knew the victim had a heart condition. She didn't say what it was, though."

Stopping in mid-stride, Singh turned to the doorway where Cross and Stone both stood and said, "Well, if that is true, it certainly could have been what killed him. Unless the victim has a brain bleed or something of that nature, these facial injuries, no matter how bad they look, are superficial and not life-threatening, much less life-ending. I will let you know something as soon as I can."

"We can't ask for anything more," Stone said as they turned and started to leave.

Almost as an afterthought, Cross made eye contact with the crime scene photographer and said, " I want pictures of every square inch of the office down the hall and of the side gate, paying particular attention to what's left of the lock."

"Will do," the photographer said.

Cross said as they walked to their car, "If we can't find anything else on our victim, then what do we do?"

"We will have to dive into every facet of his life, including his online presence, and hope we find something."

After getting back in the car and returning to the Sheriff's Department, the pair stopped at Chief Boone's office to tell him how bad the crime scene was. Then, they went straight to their cubicles to start digging into the victim's life.

Stone and Cross spent the next hour or more checking multiple databases they can access, calling the Tax Accessor's Office and the County Recorder's Office. Finally, after sitting on hold for nearly fifteen minutes, Cross hit paydirt at the Register of Deeds Office for Lexington County.

While Stone was sitting at her desk focused on her search, she suddenly perked up when she heard Cross say, "Perfect! Thank you!" before hanging up his desk phone.

"Whatcha got?" Stone asked.

Cross let out a huge smile, showing his perfect teeth, and said, "I have an address."

"Excellent! Let's go!" Stone replied as she hopped up from her chair.

Cross and Stone turned off St. Andrews Road onto Carriage Lane twenty minutes later. They had only traveled several hundred feet down the road when the GPS told them to turn into the parking lot.

Stone parked near the front door, and they both got out and walked up to the door of a plain, nondescript-looking building. No signage was posted to tell anyone what kind of establishment they were walking up to.

"You sure we're at the right place?" Stone asked, unsure.

"The lady I spoke with at the Register of Deed's Office said Michael Hawkins built and owned this building. And according to the same woman, it is registered as office space."

"Well, let's take a look around," Stone said.

They walked up to the front, where Cross tried to open the door but found it locked. "I'm going to go around the back and see if there's another way in," Stone said. "I'll be right back."

"While you do that, I'm going to call the boss and see about getting us a digital warrant for the property if we can find a way in," Cross replied.

"Good idea," Stone said as she started to walk the perimeter of the small building.

A couple of minutes later, Stone returned from the opposite way she had left, shrugged her shoulders, and said, "There's another door in back, but it's locked too."

"Of course it is," Cross chuckled, "Why make our jobs easy? I called the boss, and we should have a digital warrant in about an hour. In the meantime, how are we getting in?"

Stone thought momentarily and said, "The department has a vetted locksmithing company they use for just such an occasion. I will call them, and by the time they get here, the warrant should also be here, and we'll be ready to make entry."

"You have a locksmith company on retainer?" Cross asked with surprise.

"Pretty much," Stone said, "You seem shocked."

"Sure are. Back home in Alabama, they would call me if they needed to get through a door." Cross said with a wink as he flexed his huge arms.

"Easy there, killer," Stone said as she patted Cross on his massive shoulder, "have an ego much?"

"I'm just saying it would be faster, that's all," Cross said.

"Yeah, I know, but we don't have the warrant, and we have to secure the business when we're done, too."

Cross made a pouty expression and said, "You're no fun."

After sitting there for the next thirty minutes, Cross's phone dinged. Cross opened the new email, smiled, and said, "We have a digital warrant for the premises, so when the locksmith arrives, we can make entry."

"Perfect," Stone said with a smile.

Twenty minutes later, a white van pulled into the parking lot and parked beside their car.

Stone and Cross watched as a skinny man hopped out of the van and walked over to where they were standing. The man shook hands with Stone and Cross, then said, "My name's Caleb, and I understand you have a problem."

Cross and Stone showed their badges, and Cross said, "We need to gain entry into this business. We can show you the warrant if you need to see it."

"Nope. We're all good," Caleb said as he ignored Cross and focused his gaze on Stone, smiling.

Snapping his fingers to re-direct the locksmith, Cross said, "I'm over here. I'm the one talking to you, not my partner."

"Oh, pardon me. I'm sorry," Caleb said, "it's just that I have never seen such a pretty detective before."

"How long will it take?" Cross asked, rolling his eyes.

Caleb walked over, examined the door and locking mechanism, smiled, and said, "Piece of cake. I'll have the door opened in less than ten minutes."

Caleb walked back to the back of his van for a moment, then returned with a small tool bag and set it down by the door to begin his work. Stone and Cross watched as the locksmith worked, and true to his word, Caleb smiled as he swung the door open ten minutes later.

"Thank you," Stone said sheepishly as Caleb smiled at her as if he were showing off for her.

"Anytime for you," Caleb said as he reached into his pocket and tried to hand her a business card.

Cross snatched it from Caleb's hand and said, "I'll take that. I need it for the report. Is the lock still in working order?"

Caleb looked dejected at Cross's intercepting his business card and said, "It will be by the time you leave."

"Good," Cross said as he and Stone entered the office.

The lights came on automatically as Stone and Cross explored the first two small rooms in the office. "What was that about?" Stone asked.

"What was what about?" Cross asked, trying to brush off the question, knowing what she meant.

"Snatching that guy's card out of his hand for the report, huh? Get protective much?" Stone said, grinning.

With a huff, Cross said, "Look, the last guy that looked at you like that turned out to be a deranged killer who kicked my ass and was a few minutes away from putting a bullet in my head, so ... no. Not on my watch."

Stone giggled and said, "Ok, fair enough."

Working their way down the hallway, they came to a locked door, "Whatcha wanna bet that this is the office we've been looking for?" Stone asked.

"No bet," Cross replied.

Stone tried to open the door but found it locked. "Hang on a minute. I'm going to get the locksmith before he leaves."

"Oh, no, you're not!" Cross smirked, "I will get him while you stay here."

Stone giggled and said, "Okay, okay! I get it."

Cross walked outside and caught the locksmith just as he was packing up to leave. "Hey, we have another door we need you to get in."

"Okay, sure, no problem," Caleb replied as he took his toolbox back out of his vehicle, "lead the way."

After following Cross inside and down the hallway, Stone asked, "How long before you can get us inside the office?"

Again, Caleb looked the door over and said, "Usually, a job like this would take ten to fifteen minutes ... but for you, pretty lady, I can have you inside in five minutes."

Cross took a half-step closer to Caleb and said sternly, "You know I have a gun, right."

"Yeah, yeah," Caleb said, "I got you," as he set his tool bag down and went to work yet again.

True to his word, the door swung open five minutes later. Before Caleb could say anything, Cross said, "That will be all. Thank you."

"I'll take that as my cue to leave," Caleb said as he packed up his tools and started to leave.

"Wait a minute," Cross said, "Since this is now part of an active investigation, I have to escort you out."

"Yeah ... sure ya do," the locksmith replied as he walked toward the front door with Cross on his heels.

Cross watched him leave the premises and then returned to the locked office where he had left Stone. As he walked back down the hallway, Cross saw that Stone was still standing at the doorway, waiting for him to return.

"You ready?" Cross asked.

"Yep. Let's see what we have," Stone replied as they entered the office together.

At first glance, everything appeared to be in place. It was a normal-looking office until Cross walked around the back of the desk and found several drawers that had been pried open with some form of hand tool, probably a large screwdriver. "What have we here?" Cross said as he looked at the bent locking mechanism of the now open drawer.

While he gently looked at the remaining drawer contents, he said, "There doesn't seem to be anything here. Why would someone go through all the trouble?"

"I'm not sure, but we need to figure this out. I feel like the reason Michael Hawkins is dead is somewhere in this office," Stone said.

"I know what you mean," Cross replied. "If he was an art broker, could it have been some kind of art theft?"

"I don't think so," Stone replied, "because his house was loaded with artwork and other valuables, and nothing was taken, which leads me to believe whoever killed him was looking for something very specific."

Cross looked around the office momentarily, then walked over to a series of built-in bookshelves to examine them closer. After going over the bookshelf and opening several drawers in a nearby filing cabinet, Cross heard Stone say, "Ah-ha! I found something!"

Cross looked over to see that Stone had moved the rolling chair out of the way and was looking at the underside of the desk. Cross watched as Stone reached under the desk with both hands and pulled something free.

"What is it?" Cross asked.

As Stone took the hidden object from its hiding place, she set it on the desk and said, "Well, that's gotta mean something," Stone said as she and Cross looked at a cardboard tube that was usually used to protect posters or photographs.

"Let's open it and take a look," Cross said.

Stone removed the cover from the end of the tube and tilted one end at an angle. After giving the tube a couple of taps on the end, a rolled-up piece of canvas slid out of the tube.

"Whatcha wanna bet this is at the very center of what's going on?" Cross asked.

"No bet," Stone said as she gently unrolled the canvas. "I think we're looking at motive."

After unrolling the canvas, Stone and Cross saw it was a modern painting of a night scene of a yacht at anchor with interior lights on the yacht. The name *Omertà* could clearly be seen on the stern of the yacht. In the bottom right of the painting, where the artist usually signs their name, the letters GG written in a fancy script could be easily seen.

"I'd say there's a good probability that this is what someone was after for sure," Stone said.

Cross looked the painting over and said, "Probably. But the question is, why?"

"I have no idea," Stone said as she looked around the rest of the office, "Do you see anything wrong with this place?"

Cross stopped what he was doing and took a hard look around. After a moment, he snapped his fingers and said, "There's no computer!"

"Exactly. Not a computer, printer, hard drive, or even unplugged cords that would indicate there ever was a computer here," Stone said.

"Meaning what exactly?" Cross asked.

"Meaning, if this guy was some kind of art broker ... where's the rest of the art?"

"That's a damn good question," Cross said with a huff.

"At any rate, we need to get someone from the crime scene unit over here to dust for prints, take photos, and see if they can find anything. Maybe we'll get lucky."

"I doubt it," Cross replied. "Remember, all the doors were locked, and there were no visible signs of a break-in from the outside, meaning whoever did this—"

"Was good," Stone finished.

"Hopefully, the crime scene guys can get a print or give us something to go on because right now, we don't have anything at all," Cross replied.

"Tell me about it," Stone huffed, "as of now, we have a murder, home invasion, and burglary all tied together, and we have zip for suspects or a motive for that matter."

"The boss is not going to like this," Cross said as he called the department to get someone to come to their location and dust for prints.

"We do at least have something to go on anyway. Whatever is going on has got to have something to do with that painting we found." Stone replied.

"Yeah, I'd be surprised if it didn't. Now we have to figure out what it means," Cross said.

3

Stone and Cross spent the rest of the afternoon at Michael Hawkins' office, thoroughly examining it while cataloging anything with even a hint of importance, which obviously included the hidden painting they found.

While they were doing that, two people from the crime scene unit were there working in tandem with the two detectives, photographing evidence and collecting fingerprints from the office space.

Once the detectives and the two people from the crime scene unit were finished, they secured the front door just as people left the business next door. While Stone and Cross were thanking the two crime scene officers for coming to help, a gentleman walked into the parking lot from the business next door. He said, "We've seen you guys over here this afternoon. I understand if you can't tell me much, but is Michael okay?"

Ignoring the question for the moment, Cross asked, "So, I take it you know Mr. Hawkins?"

"Oh, yeah, we often play golf together. He's a really nice guy."

"You know him pretty well then?" Stone asked.

"Sure, I'd say so. We've been friends for years. Why? What's going on? Is Michael in some trouble?"

Stone said, "Can you tell us exactly what Mr. Hawkins did for a living?"

"You mean you don't know?" the man asked.

Cross said, "I'm afraid we don't know exactly what he does. We know it has something to do with art and artwork, but that's all."

"He's an art broker," the man said, "from what Michael told me, he buys and sells artwork and brings prospective buyers and sellers together for a fee."

"I see," Stone said. "And what is your name?"

"My name is Billy Avila. I work at the insurance company next door," the newcomer said as he shook hands with Stone and Cross.

"I'm afraid we can't give you any details because it's an ongoing investigation," Cross said, "but we are curious ... do you happen to know if he has any other locations anywhere?"

The man rubbed his chin momentarily and said, "Let me think ... nope, just this office and his home. Oh, wait! I don't know if it's what you're looking for, but once, he took me to see his collection of artwork."

"And where was this?" Stone asked inquisitively.

"As I remember, it was called ... Everguard Self-Storage."

"Perfect. Thank you." Stone said as she wrote down the name of the storage facility.

As Stone and Cross turned and started to walk off, the man asked, "Can you at least tell me if Michael is okay?"

Cross looked at Stone and replied, "I'm sorry, but he's not okay. I can't tell you any more than that."

After finally pulling out of the parking lot, Stone said, "Let's get this painting under lock and key, then call it a day so we can start fresh in the morning."

∾

THE FOLLOWING MORNING, Cross and Stone arrived at the department simultaneously and walked in together. "Did you get some sleep last night?" Stone asked.

"Sure did. I ate, watched TV, and was in bed at nine o'clock. It was pure heaven." Cross replied with a smile.

"Sounds like it," Stone said with a smile, "so I was thinking about what to do next in the case, and I'm thinking we need to go visit Everguard Self-Storage."

As the pair walked deeper into the building, they entered a large room full of cubicles known as the bullpen. Cross said as they wove their way to their tandem cubicle, "I was thinking. A self-storage facility doesn't seem like the best place to store an art collection."

"I had the same thought, which is why after I got home last night, I checked out their website," Stone said.

"And what did you find?"

"In short, they are a self-storage facility for high-end items. The website says they have hermetically sealed, climate-controlled rooms for rent that are essentially walk-in safes."

"Now it makes sense," Cross replied.

"Yeah, so we will definitely need a warrant when we pay them a visit." Stone said.

"Not a problem. I'll take care of it," Cross said with a wink as both settled into their cubicle.

Before Cross could begin the paperwork, the phone on Stone's desk started to ring. "Oh, shit. That's never a good sign when the phone rings this early," Stone said.

Pausing to take a deep breath before answering the phone, Stone picked the receiver up and said, "Stone here." Cross watched Stone's body language as she rolled her eyes and shook her head simultaneously, indicating she was not happy about what she heard. Stone said, "But we're in the middle of a case already ... yes, boss."

Stone hung up the phone, grabbed her temples, and said, "It's going to be one of those days. Let's go. We have another case."

"Wait, what do you mean we have another case?" Cross replied, shocked, "Doesn't he know we're hip-deep in this one already?"

"Oh, he knows. He also knows everyone else has more active cases than we do, so we get another one," Stone said as both grabbed their notepads and left their cubicle five minutes after arriving.

"My butt hadn't even warmed the seat up yet," Cross said with a smirk, "so where are we going?"

"Your favorite place," Stone said with an evil grin.

"Oh, shit ... don't tell me," Cross said.

"Yep. There's a body at the lake."

"Is it too late for me to make a sick call?" Cross asked.

"Uh, yeah," Stone said as she smacked him on his massive shoulder.

As they retraced their steps back to the parking lot, Coss said, "So, where exactly are we going?"

Stone smirked and said, "You'll see."

"Aw man, it's too early for this mess today," Cross said in his patent Alabama drawl.

She giggled as they got into Stone's car, saying, "It's ok. We won't need to get on a boat, so you don't have to worry your pretty little head."

Cross glanced at Stone and said, "Look, I haven't had my coffee yet. It's too early for that shit."

Stone let out an evil laugh and said, "Aw, did the big pouty man not get his coffee this morning?"

As Stone pulled out of the parking lot, Cross smiled and said, "Keep playing, ya hear, and the next time we get out of this car, the big pouty man's gonna kick your behind."

Stone couldn't help but laugh at Cross's statement. Even though they had been working together for less than a year, they simply clicked like best friends, making the two detectives quite the pair on the professional level and the best of friends away from work.

"You gonna let me off the hook are what? Where are we going?" Cross prodded.

"Relax, big man. We're going to a body recovery on Pine Island."

"So, you're sure, no boats then?" Cross inquired.

"Nope. Not as far as I know. From what I've heard, a body was seen earlier floating in the water just off Pine Island. A department rescue boat and the dive team are there already. The boss wants us to be there when it's recovered, and the coroner is already en route."

As Stone drove, Cross asked, "So, about yesterday, what do you think that painting we found means?"

"I don't know but it has to mean something just by the very fact that it was hidden like it was," Stone replied. "Try looking up *Omertà* and see what it means. Maybe that will tell us something."

In less than a minute, Cross had typed the yacht's name into his phone and stared at the results, "That's not good," Cross said.

"What's not good?" Stone asked inquisitively.

"Yeah ... the name Omertà is Italian for 'code of silence,'" Cross said.

"Aw shit," Stone groaned, "that's not good at all."

"So, we're thinking the same thing then?" Cross asked.

"Let's not make things out to be worse than they appear ... yet," Stone said, "but the phrase code of silence screams mob."

"My thoughts exactly," Cross replied as they crossed the Lake Murray Dam, indicating they were getting close to the body recovery site.

After crossing the dam, Stone turned left onto North Lake Drive and followed the GPS down River Road until they saw a sign that read Pine Island Road. After traveling less than a quarter mile, they pulled onto a small causeway leading to the island.

"Okay, we're here. Now, where do we go?" Cross asked.

"Not sure, but the island is not that big, so we'll take a loop around and see what we see," Stone replied.

They had gone less than one hundred yards when Cross pointed off to their right and said, "There are a couple of squad cars over there, and there's a sheriff's boat right offshore."

Stone drove over as close as she could before having to stop. Both got out and started towards the two deputies standing at the shoreline, watching the sheriff's boat not more than twenty-five yards offshore.

"What's going on?" Cross said to the two deputies as they showed their badges.

"I'm not entirely sure yet," one of the deputies replied. "We were dispatched to check out something that could be a body floating just off Pine Island ... dispatch said an anonymous caller called it in."

The other deputy piped in and said, "Yeah, my partner and I were sent over to check it out and saw something near where the sheriff's boat is now ... possibly a woman in a dress is what it looked like. We called for the sheriff's boat and dive team, but by the time they arrived, the body had apparently sunk."

"Wonderful," Cross replied, unenthused about the prospect of sitting around while the dive team did their search.

Cross and Stone had been there approximately ten minutes when they heard another vehicle approaching the area. Upon seeing the coroner's vehicle pulling up, Stone looked over her shoulder and said, "The gang's all here."

"Oh, goody, goody," Cross said while bobbing his head from side to side, trying to imitate the Lexington County Coroner, Dr. Sandeep Singh.

A few minutes later, Dr. Singh walked up with a couple of his assistant coroners and asked, "What do we have?"

Stone shrugged and said, "Not sure. Divers have not recovered a body yet."

"So, it's a waiting game then," Singh replied.

"Exactly," Cross said as Stone caught him checking out one of the assistant coroners.

"Maybe not," Stone said excitedly as she pointed into the lake where the divers were in the water.

All three watched as first one diver appeared, then the second with what appeared to be a body. Moments later, the deputy who stayed on the boat radioed one of the deputies to have the detectives meet them at the small dock approximately one hundred yards further down the shore from where they were located.

Cross, Stone, and Singh walked the short distance to the dock, but before he left, Singh had his two assistant coroners move their vehicle closer so they would not have to move the remains any further than they had to. While they walked, Cross asked, "So, uh, Dr. Singh, who's the new assistant? I don't believe I've seen her before."

"I should hope not," Singh replied. "She's a new transfer. She is a lovely young lady and very capable of performing her job."

"I'm sure she can," Stone replied as she shot a sly smile at Cross.

Cross saw Stone grinning at him and said, "What?" as he tried to play it off.

Singh also caught on and said, "I just happen to know that she is new to the area and does not have any friends here, nor does she have a significant other."

"Interesting, very interesting," Cross said.

A few minutes later, as the three walked onto the short dock, they heard the sheriff's boat crank and start in their direction. It would only be a few more minutes before they saw the remains firsthand. As the sheriff's boat came closer, Dr. Singh took a small vial of ointment out of his pocket, rubbed a little under his nostrils, and passed it to Stone, who did the same and passed it on to Cross.

"What is it?" Cross asked.

"Vicks vapor rub," Singh replied, "it will help with the odor."

Cross did the same as Stone and Singh, replaced the cap, and tossed the small vial back to Singh, "Thanks for that," Cross said.

"What's a little professional courtesy between co-workers," Singh replied. "Prepare yourselves. If these remains have been in the water for a while, they could be quite foul."

"Oh, lovely," Cross replied as the sheriff's boat pulled up.

Stone made eye contact with one of the divers she knew and said, "Hey, Jansen. Whatcha got for us?"

The diver who had pulled the body out of the water replied, "Looks like you got a fresh one. Couldn't have been in the water too long."

Without waiting for Singh's orders, the two assistant coroners boarded the sheriff's boat and retrieved the remains that had already been placed in a body bag by the two divers.

After retrieving the body bag as carefully as possible, the two assistant coroners placed the remains on a gurney they had brought with them. Before strapping the remains down, Singh unzipped the bag and did a quick examination, saying, "It's a female whose age is approximately mid-twenties. I'd say she hasn't been in the water for more than ... two days. I won't be sure until I get her back to autopsy."

"Any signs of a struggle?" Stone asked.

"None that I can see right offhand," Singh replied.

"Is that an evening dress?" Cross asked, even though he already knew the answer.

"Indeed it is," Singh replied, "and might I say quite a stunning shade of emerald at that. She apparently had quite the eye for color because the beige heels were paired perfectly. I might add that the entire outfit goes perfectly with her stunning red hair."

Stone looked out onto the lake and muttered to no one in particular, "Now, just where in the hell did you come from?"

As Cross was about to ask a question, Stone and Cross saw the quizzical look on Singh's face. "What is it?" Stone asked.

Singh shook his head as he stared at the fingers of the remains and said, "I'm not sure yet, but it *looks* like whoever this was attempted to obliterate her fingerprints."

"You can do that?" Cross asked, shocked.

"You would be surprised at what lengths people will go to keep their identity hidden," Singh replied.

"How can you tell someone tried to alter their fingerprints?" Stone asked.

"There are multiple cuts on each fingertip in different directions which, although rudimentary, is very effective at altering the fingerprints."

"Could it have been a form of cutting or self-mutilation?" Stone asked.

Tilting his head slightly as if weighing what Stone asked, Singh replied, "I can't rule it out, but, in this case, I'd say it's not likely. The cuts do not appear to have been done to inflict pain, which is the purpose of people who self-harm." After pausing briefly, Singh continued, "No, I'd stake my reputation on it that this was an attempt to destroy their fingerprints and nothing more."

"Thank you, doctor," Stone replied.

Singh nodded and said, "I will let you know as soon as I have something for you."

"Thank you," Stone said as she turned and started walking off. After a few steps, she noticed Cross was still standing near the body, "ya, coming?" she asked, knowing full and well what he was doing.

"I'll be there in a minute," Cross replied. "I … uh, I want to check one more thing."

"Yeah, sure ya do," Stone said, smiling, and started walking back to the car.

A few moments later, Cross caught up with Stone and started walking beside her, grinning from ear to ear. Stone looked at him, and he said sheepishly, "What?"

"Did ya get it?" Stone asked.

"Get what?" Cross asked innocently.

"You know what," Stone blurted out.

"I have no idea what you're talking about," Cross said, smiling from ear to ear.

Stone said as the pair returned to the car, "Anyway, we have yet another body with nothing to go on, and you're not getting off that easy. Did you get her phone number or not?"

"Well, I gave her my phone number. She said she would text me her number. I have no idea if she will or not, but that's what she said, and I wouldn't be too sure about not having anything to go on with the body either," Cross replied.

"Why do you say that?" Stone asked.

Once they reached the car, Cross said, "Get in, and I'll tell you."

After turning around and driving back across the causeway, Stone said, "Ok, spill it. Whatcha got?"

Before Cross could reply, his phone dinged. He glanced at his phone to see a phone number and the name—Yasmin.

Cross smiled from ear to ear, and Stone said, "You got it! You old sly dog, you!"

Cross looked at her while she drove, smiled devilishly, and said, "It would appear so. Anyway, it's all about the dress. She dressed classy for a night out but not to a nightclub or bar. As Singh pointed out, with the high heels, she was either at or going somewhere ritzy. So, the question is ... where?"

"Well, there aren't too many places around the lake that fit that bill. There are a couple of restaurants in the Ballentine area and ..." Stone said as her voice trailed off.

"And what?" Cross asked.

"And I might know where she came from," Stone said as she snapped her fingers.

"Enlighten me. Oh, great wise one," Cross said with a snicker.

Ignoring Cross's comment, Stone said, "There's a yacht based in Ballentine called *The Spirit of Lake Murray*. This yacht is a dinner cruise and special event kind of place. It could be that she fell overboard from the cruise."

Cross wrinkled his face, shook his head, and said, "Nah, I don't believe it. Unless this was a huge ship with several hundred people onboard ... wouldn't they realize someone fell overboard?"

"I have no idea, really, but it's at least worth checking out. It could explain how the body ended up where it did, or I could be way off base. I just don't know," Stone said, "but let's say, for argument's sake, the victim was at a fancy dockside restaurant; somebody would have seen her fall in or heard her splashing around. Not to mention, if that's the case, how did she end up way out here near Pine Island, where there are no fancy restaurants around?"

"Good point," Cross admitted.

"Now, if she were on a dinner cruise and somehow ended up in the water, she would only be visible for a few seconds before she disappeared into the darkness of the lake," Stone suggested.

"I see your point," Cross said. "So, where can we find this yacht?"

Stone thought momentarily and said, "I believe it docks in Ballentine across the dam. If that's true, it means, technically, it's out of our jurisdiction and in Richland County. Usually, though, we can call the boss, and he'll make a phone call, and we're good."

Cross said, "Start heading that way then, and I'll call the boss."

Stone grinned and said, "I like your style. And after that, you need to call Yasmin and ask her out on a date!"

4

Before long, Stone and Cross pulled into the parking area for *The Spirit of Lake Murray* and got out. As they approached the dock where the yacht was tied up, a middle-aged man missing the lower portion of his left arm saw them coming and said, "Sorry folks, *The Spirit's* not running today."

Cross and Stone smiled and said, "We're not here for a tour. We're Lexington County Sheriff's Detectives and need to ask someone a few questions. Is the owner around?"

"Right now, I'd say you're looking at him. My name is Rick Crout, and I'm part owner of the Spirit. How can I help you?"

"We're not sure if you can, but we're hoping you have some information that might be useful for us," Stone replied.

"Oh, and in what way?"

Stone asked, "When did you last take your boat for a cruise?"

"That would have been the night before last," Crout said, "why? What's going on?"

Stone cautiously replied, "We are investigating a body pulled from the lake this morning. Her manner of dress indicates she was either going to or at a high-priced event or party."

Before Crout could reply, Cross added, "Would it be possible for someone to fall overboard from your yacht without someone noticing?"

Without missing a beat, Crout replied, "On the lake, anything's possible, but … it's not very likely. *The Spirit* is a big yacht, but it's not that big. I find it hard to believe that someone could go overboard without another gust seeing unless—" his voice trailing off mid-sentence.

"Unless what?" Cross asked.

Rubbing his chin, Rick thought for a minute, then said, "The last night we went out, there was a minor problem aboard *The Spirit*."

"Okay, you have our interest," Stone replied.

"I can't see where that would have anything to do with a woman in the lake, though," Crout replied.

"How about telling us anyway," Stone replied sternly.

Crout nodded and replied, "On our last trip, about an hour out from the dock, everyone onboard started smelling a burning smell. It wasn't long before a cloud of smoke could be seen hanging around. As it turns out, there was a minor fire in the men's room. People started to panic a little, but the crew put the fire out with no problem. Since the smell was thick in the air and people were slightly unnerved, we thought it best to return to the dock and air out *The Spirit*."

"So, with what was going on … it is possible that someone went overboard and wasn't seen?" Cross asked.

"I guess it's possible," Crout replied, "if I had a little more context, I might be able to help more, although I was mainly in the wheelhouse."

"Do you serve beer and wine?" Cross asked.

"Yes, we have a full bar and a pretty spectacular galley and kitchen staff, if I do say so myself," Crout replied proudly.

"Can you give us a list of the waitstaff and their contact information?" Stone asked.

"Sure, no problem," Crout replied, "I'll be right back."

"What do you think?" Stone asked Cross as Crout went to get the list.

"It sounds like someone intentionally started a fire as a distraction. That's what I think." Cross replied.

Stone raised an eyebrow and said, "It fits, that's for sure."

A few minutes later, Crout returned, handed Cross a sheet of paper, and said, "These are the only waitstaff we have. I also added the bartender too."

"Perfect, thanks," Cross replied.

As Stone and Cross turned to leave, Crout asked, "You don't really think she fell off *The Spirit*? Do you?"

Stone stopped and said, "Honestly, we're not sure of anything right now. We could be in touch again at a later date. Thank you."

"We'll be here," Crout said as the pair started walking toward Stone's car.

As they got into the car, Cross asked, "So, who's up first?"

"Somebody named Chris Fox. He does not live far away from here."

"Lead the way," Cross replied.

It took the duo about fifteen minutes to reach the address given to them earlier by one of the part-owners of *The Spirit of Lake Murray.*

They pulled into the driveway of the older yet neatly kept home and parked.

"Let's go have a chat with Chris," Cross said.

The always cautious pair walked up to the front door, checking the windows to ensure they were not surprised. Cross knocked on the door, took a step back, and waited. Within moments, they could hear footsteps coming to the door, and suddenly the door opened. A middle-aged man with long, dark brown, unkempt hair opened the door, obviously expecting someone else.

The man took one look at the badges on Stone and Cross's waist and said, "Oh, shit! Cops!" The as-yet-unidentified man turned to run and attempted to slam the door in Cross's face. Without hesitation, Cross bounded through the door and tackled the man with all the conviction of a defensive end sacking a quarterback.

Both men went down in a heap in the doorway leading from the front room into the hallway, "Geeze, dude! Take it easy! The man said as Cross pinned him down to the ground and easily manhandled the as yet unidentified man, putting cuffs on him in a matter of seconds.

Just as Cross was getting the cuffs on the male, a wild-eyed female came into view, yelling, "What's going on?"

Stone drew her service weapon, aimed it at the new threat, and yelled, "GET BACK!"

The woman, who was every bit of one hundred and twenty pounds, immediately stopped in her tracks and threw her hands up wild-eyed, "Don't shoot!"

"BACK UP!" Stone commanded sternly.

The visibly shaken woman complied, backed up, and watched as Cross snatched the man off the floor into a seated position. "Chris Fox, I presume?"

"Uh, no. My name's Tony ... Tony Mecanna," the young man said.

Cross looked at Stone, confused, and asked, "Why did you run then?"

The young man looked at the floor, hesitated momentarily, and said, "I panicked because I have weed in my pocket."

Before either detective could respond, the young woman said, "I'm actually Chris. Why do you want me?"

"First off, do you have anything on you?" Stone asked as she approached the young woman.

"No," the woman replied as Stone cautiously put her in handcuffs for the time being and patted the woman down.

Cross stood the man up who attempted to run, patted him down to ensure he had no weapons, and removed the small baggie of a green leafy substance from his pocket.

Cross examined the small baggie and said, "Really, dude? That's why you tried to run."

"I'm sorry. Like I said, I panicked," the visibly shaken young man replied as Cross and Stone sat both of them on the couch.

"Honestly, we could care less about the baggie of weed," Stone snapped, "We're homicide detectives and—"

"HOMICIDE!" The man named Tony nearly yelled, "Whoa! Wait a minute, I smoke a little weed every now and then, but I don't know anything about a homicide. Who got killed?"

Ignoring the question at first, Stone and Cross got both of their ID's to ensure what they were saying was true. After verifying the woman was indeed the "Chris" they were looking for, Stone said, "As I was attempting to say, we're homicide cops, and we are investigating a suspicious death on the lake, and we were hoping that you, Chris, might know something."

"Me?" the young woman, whose full name was Christiana, asked, "I don't know anything about a murder."

"Maybe you do and just don't know it," Cross said.

"What do you mean?" The young woman asked.

"Are you a waitress onboard *The Spirit of Lake Murray*?" Stone asked.

"Yes, why?" The visibly shaken woman replied.

Stone said, "The last night out, did you see anything unusual?"

The still-shaking woman thought for a moment and said, "Do you mean the fire? I think that was an accident. I remember one of the crew saying something about a cigarette butt being found in the trashcan or something."

Cross interjected, trying to redirect the young woman, "We know about the fire. Is there anything else you can think of that happened that night?"

"I really can't think of anything," Chris replied hesitantly.

Stone replied sternly, "Look, I can tell you know something. Either you tell us what it is, or we're going to take your boyfriend in for drug possession."

Wild-eyed, the man now known as Tony said, "TELL THEM!"

"Tell us what?" Cross prodded.

"I don't know for certain. I don't want to get anybody into trouble," Chris said, her voice quivering.

"Okay, okay," Chris replied, "I'll tell you, but I don't know what happened, okay," she again reiterated.

"Fine. Just tell us what you saw," Stone said.

"The night the yacht caught fire, there was a woman onboard eating dinner by herself, which was unusual because The Spirit is the type of place where you come for a dinner date or with other couples. This woman came alone. She asked me if I had seen anyone else alone onboard."

"And did you?"

"As a matter of fact, yes. I told her there was a man on the upper deck near the stern that was alone."

"And what did she say to that?" Stone asked as Cross wrote everything down.

The woman replied something like, "I can't believe I missed him. I'll go up in a bit. But ..." her voice trailed off as if she were thinking intently about something.

"What is it?" Stone prodded, glancing at Cross.

"But that's when the fire happened, and I don't remember seeing the woman again after the fire. I can't believe I just now thought about that."

"It's because you were distracted by the smoke and fire," Cross said.

"I guess, but thinking back ... I don't remember seeing her get off the ship either. It's not uncommon, but I would have remembered her."

"Oh, and why's that?" Stone asked.

"I remember because she was carrying a sketchbook, wearing a beautiful green dress, and man! I'd kill to have her red hair!"

Stone and Cross's eyes widened upon hearing this, and before they could say anything, Chris said, "Wait! Not literally. That was a poor choice of words."

"We figured," Stone replied, "Do you remember what the man looked like?"

"Vaguely. He was dressed a little more casually than the others, but he was handsome, had dark, almost jet-black hair, and a slightly darker complexion."

Cross asked, "Was he Spanish?"

"Definitely not," the girl replied, "If I had to guess, I'd say Greek, Italian maybe, or at least from the Mediterranean."

"Oh, and just why do you think that?" Cross asked.

"Because I've always wanted to go to Greece, and I watch videos online all the time about that area of the world, and the man on board has those same kinds of features."

"I see," Cross replied as he wrote everything down.

Stone asked, "Is there anything else you can think of?"

Shaking her head, the woman said, "No, that's everything."

Stone said, "Wait a minute. Go back for a second. You said the woman had a sketchbook?"

"Yeah, she did. Before the sun went down, I saw her sketching the sunset from the upper deck before she found a seat on the lower deck."

"Did you see what happened to the sketchbook?" Stone asked. "Think. This could be very important."

Deep in thought, the young woman sat there for a few seconds and said, "Wait! I remember! I saw Captain Rick with it after everyone disembarked."

While Stone and Cross took the cuffs off the pair, Cross looked at the young man named Tony and said, "Today's your lucky day. If we weren't in the middle of a big case, you'd be taking a ride with me."

The young man nodded, mumbled thanks, and sat back on the couch.

After leaving the two, Cross and Stone walked outside to their car, and Cross said, "I bet I know where we're going now."

"Exactly," Stone replied, "back to *The Spirit of Lake Murray*."

"Do you think we need to talk to anybody on the list who may have been working onboard that night?"

"Not just yet," Stone replied, "we may have all we need."

~

As THEY PULLED into the parking lot of *The Spirit of Lake Murray* again for the second time in less than an hour, Cross said, "Oh, look, we're back again."

Captain Rick heard the car pull up, walked out on deck, and asked, "Back so soon?"

"Looks that way," Stone said as they exited the car and walked onto the dock where *The Spirit of Lake Muray* was tied up.

Cross said, "We just finished interviewing Chris, and she said something about a sketchbook being found, and you had it after everyone disembarked. Do you still have it?"

"I sure do. I was hoping someone would realize they didn't have it and come looking for it. Do you think it's important?"

"It could be. Can you get it for us?" Stone asked.

"Sure, be right back," Rick replied.

Rick walked inside the yacht for a few minutes, then reappeared with a sketchbook about the size of a standard notebook. "Here ya go," Rick said, smiling as he handed the sketchpad to Cross.

Without even looking at it, Cross said, "Thank you for this. It could prove very useful."

"No problem. Glad I could help," Rick said as he watched them return to their car.

Before Stone turned the car around, Cross opened the sketchbook and thumbed through the pages. He saw over a dozen sketches in various degrees of completion as he went through the pages. "It looks like whoever owned this sketchbook would work on a sketch for a while, then move on to another." Cross said, "The finished ones are actually quite good."

As Stone drove, she heard Cross in the passenger's seat say, "Oh, shit ... we have a problem."

"I don't like the sound of that," Stone said as she glanced over at Cross, "What do you see?"

"You're not going to believe it," Cross replied, shocked.

"Why?"

"The finished sketches in this book are signed GG, exactly like the hidden painting we found at Michael Hawkin's office."

Stone asked, "Could it be that the artist GG and the woman in the emerald dress are one and the same?"

"Either that or this is one hell of a coincidence," Cross replied.

"I don't believe in coincidences," Stone snapped.

"Neither do I," Cross replied. "Let's get back to the department and look at this again from the beginning. We need to make sure they are the same person."

5

After returning to the department and taking a seat in their cubicles, which they called their "home away from home," they went over everything again from the top.

For the next hour, the duo created a timeline of events as they understood them on a large whiteboard hanging across the back wall of their shared cubicle.

After they examined the timeline of events, Cross said, "We need to see what's in that high-end self-storage unit, and we really need to figure out who this woman is we just fished out of the lake."

"I agree," Stone replied. After sitting silently for a moment, Stone looked at Cross and suggested, "Divide and conquer?"

"Sound's good to me," Cross replied, "I'll take the self-storage place."

"And while you do that, I'll go pay Doctor Singh a visit and see if he has anything on the young lady in the emerald dress," Stone replied.

As both pushed their chairs back and got up, Chief of Detectives Stephen Boone walked up and asked, "Where are you two going?"

After giving Boone a brief synopsis of what was happening and why they thought the two cases might be linked, Boone said, "Well, don't let me stop you. Get at it."

"Roger that," Cross said as they started for the door.

HALF AN HOUR LATER, Cross pulled up to the property owned and operated by Everguard Self-Storage. After turning off the main road, Cross stopped at a callbox with a numbered keypad, a camera lens, and a call button.

Cross pushed the call button, and shortly, a voice asked, "Can I help you?"

Cross held his badge to the camera and replied, "Yes, I'm Detective Raylon Cross with the Lexington County Sheriff's Department. I need to speak with someone in charge, please."

The disembodied voice replied, "Please pull through, find a parking spot, and someone will come to meet you."

Cross pulled into the first available parking spot and got out. As he walked to the back of his car, he retrieved a pair of gloves, several evidence bags, and a roll of crime scene tape as a precaution as a security guard approached and introduced himself. "I'm Pete, and I'm in charge of the facility at the moment. What can I do for you?"

Cross replied, "I'm here with a warrant. I need to see inside one particular vault owned by Michael Hawkins."

"I know, Mr. Hawkins," the guard replied, smiling. "I hope everything's okay. He's one of the nice ones."

Cross said, "I wish I could say, but all I can say is that it's an ongoing investigation. Can you show me and open his vault, please?"

"Sure, no problem. We need to stop by the office so I can make a copy of the warrant, and we'll be good," the guard replied.

"Lead the way," Cross replied.

After stopping at the office for the guard to make a copy of the warrant, the guard escorted Cross down a corridor with what were essentially high-dollar self-storage units. "How much do these things cost a month?" Cross asked.

"More than I can afford, that's for sure," the guard said with a laugh.

"That's kinda what I was thinking, too. Rich people and their toys," Cross said with a huff.

"Exactly," the guard replied as he stopped at one of the doors. "This is Mr. Hawkins's unit."

"Open it, please," Cross said.

The guard took out his ID card and held it up to the lock. After two seconds, they both heard an audible click and a slight hiss of air as the hefty door unlocked.

"Thank you. Please stand back." Cross said, glancing at the guard.

Cross slid his hands into a pair of nitrile gloves in one practiced motion. A motion sensor picked up his movement when he stepped inside the room. Within one second, a light turned on, illuminating the room's interior.

Cross stood frozen in awe for several seconds before he could manage to utter, "Holy ... shit."

At least a dozen paintings were in specially built racks to prevent them from banging into one another. After looking at several paintings, it was apparent that this was where Michael Hawkins had been keeping the paintings he was brokering because, at first glance, there were several different artists' works in the room. However, one in particular stood out as being ... familiar.

After looking at several more framed pieces of artwork, Cross was sure Mr. Hawkins took a particular interest in one artist—the artist who only signed their works with the initials GG.

In the very back corner of the room was a small square table and a single chair. The table was just big enough for a few notebooks and nothing more. "Apparently, Mr. Hawkins likes to keep track of things the old-fashioned way," Cross said aloud, although he was the only person in the room.

About that time, the security guard stuck his head inside and said, "Were you talking to me, detective?" Before Cross could respond, the guard replied, saw the painting closest to him, and snapped excitedly, "That's ... that's a Gabriella Gibson painting!"

"Who's that?" Cross said, shocked.

"She's a local artist who has become quite famous in the past year or so," the guard replied excitedly.

"And just how do you know about her?" Cross asked.

"I don't, but my wife does. My wife admires her work and wants one of her paintings, but I will have to save up a little bit first."

"I'm almost afraid to ask. Are they expensive?" Cross asked.

"Not for what you get, so says my wife. I think the cheapest one sold recently for around four hundred dollars or so. I think the priciest of her paintings I've seen so far is around fifteen hundred dollars. They are not overpriced, but everyone feels certain they will go higher in the future as people snap them up."

"I see," Cross replied, "if you know so much about her, then can you tell me where she lives?"

"Nobody seems to know. She's a bit of a recluse. She doesn't do interviews or anything of that sort. Nobody even knows for certain if that is her real name or not," the guard replied from the doorway.

"Interesting. Very interesting," Cross said as he looked around for a few more minutes. Would you know her if you saw her?"

Shaking his head from side to side, the guard replied, "I don't know if anybody knows what she looks like. That's part of the allure to her paintings ... according to my wife, that is."

"I gotcha," Cross replied as he carefully put the notebooks into evidence bags and sealed them. As he slid the notebooks into an evidence bag, a slip of paper fell from between the notebooks and landed on the floor by his feet. "Hello, there. What have we here?" Cross said as he bent over and picked up the slip of paper. Turning the paper over, he saw an address written in blue pen on one side; *gonna have to check that out*, Cross thought to himself as he slipped it back into the evidence bag.

After Cross stepped outside, he told the security guard to secure the door.

Once the door was closed and secured, Cross put a large X across the door with crime scene tape. "So, I take it nobody in or out?" The guard asked.

"Exactly," Cross replied as they started walking out.

As they stopped at the front of the building, Cross shook hands with Pete and said, "You've been a big help in more ways than one."

Pete smirked and asked, "Enough of a help to get my hands on one of those paintings in there?"

"I'm afraid not. I believe they'll be evidence before this is all over," Cross replied.

Pete laughed innocently and said, "I didn't think that would work."

ONE HOUR EARLIER ACROSS LEXINGTON, Detective Stone pulled up to a small building off Duffie Drive and into the small parking lot on the side of the building. Stone walked in the front door, and a woman on the opposite side of a pass-through window slid the window open and asked, "Can I help you?"

"Yes, I'm Detective Stone, and I'm here to see Doctor Singh, please," Stone replied.

"Great, I've been waiting for you. I'll buzz you in," the woman said as a buzzing sound emanated from the door beside the pass-through window. Stone pushed on the door and walked down the hallway to where she knew Doctor Singh's office was. Stone knocked on the closed door and heard a muffled 'enter' from the other side.

When she made eye contact with Singh, he said, "Ah, Detective Stone, I was expecting you. I have some troubling results for you from the woman in the emerald dress."

"Oh, and what's that," Stone asked.

"My people have just completed the autopsy, and I can say for certain that this was no accident. She was undoubtedly murdered."

Stone sighed and said, "Somehow ... I knew you would say that. How did she die?"

Singh said, "Her official cause of death is homicide, but technically, she drowned in the lake. Upon performing the autopsy, the decedent was found to have a one-inch wide knife wound between the fourth and fifth rib on her right side. The stab wound immediately penetrated her right lung, robbing her of the ability to call for help.

She was alive when she went into the water, and we know this by the presence of lake water in her left lung. She would have died in mere seconds after going into the water."

"And that explains why she apparently never called out for help. She couldn't. By the time she realized she was under attack, it was already too late," Stone said sadly.

"Precisely," Singh replied.

Stone sat silently for a moment, then asked, "Were you able to identify her?"

"Sadly, not yet. I hate to say it, but someone did a good enough job on her fingerprints, and I can't get anything usable from them."

"What about DNA or dental records?" Stone asked.

"The woman had impeccable teeth, so they aren't going to be of much help in this instance. I have taken a DNA sample that is undergoing testing now, but as you well know, if there's nothing to match it to, it's of no real use either."

"So, what you're telling me is identifying her could be a lengthy process." Stone said.

"If there is nothing else to go on, it very well could be," Singh replied.

At that moment, Stone's phone rang. She glanced at it to see the name Cross on the display. Answering it quickly, Stone said, "I have some good news and bad news."

Unable to contain himself, Cross blurted out, "Me too! Thanks to Pete, the security guard over here ... I might know the name of the painter GG."

"That's fantastic!" Stone said excitedly.

"What's your bad news," Cross asked.

"The woman in the emerald dress, if it turns out to be the artist GG, was most definitely murdered. Dr. Singh found a stab wound between her fourth and fifth ribs on her right side, which deflated her right lung almost instantly. After that, somebody pushed her overboard."

"Damn, that's cold-blooded," Cross replied.

"Where are you now?" Stone asked.

"I am pulling out of the Everguard Self-Storage facility now, and let me tell you ... this place ain't no joke. It works like a standard storage unit company but with one exception: each unit is basically a scaled-down vault."

"Well, you can give me the scoop when we meet back up. You headed back to the department?" Stone asked.

"Yep, sure am. I want to check out this name the security guard gave me and see if it pans out."

"Okay. I will see you back there in a little while. I haven't eaten in a while, and it's past lunch. I'm going to call in an order to Creekside and swing by to pick it up before I come in. You want anything?"

"Sure!" Cross replied excitedly, "I was just thinking I was starting to get hungry too!"

"Whatcha want?" Stone asked.

"I'll have the marinated grilled chicken on a sandwich and fries!" Cross replied enthusiastically.

"Done," Stone said, "I'll be there in a little bit."

6

After Stone and Cross met at the department, Stone asked, "So, what's this mysterious GG's actual name?"

Snatching his order from Stone, Cross smiled and said, "It'll wait another few minutes!"

"Well, okay then!" Stone replied with a laugh as they both sat down at their desks and ate their late lunches.

Ten minutes later, Cross sat back in his chair, wiped his mouth with a napkin, and tossed it on his empty to-go plate, "Man! Kirt sure knows how to make a grilled chicken sandwich!" Cross said with a smile.

"Yes, he does, and his cheeseburgers are just as good as any around," Stone said with a wink, "so, tell me, who is this mysterious artist GG?"

"Well, according to the security guard whom I talked to today, "GG is actually Gabriella Gibson, a reclusive artist living in the area."

"What was in the Everguard Self-Storage unit?" Stone asked.

Cross said, "It was essentially what we thought. There were probably a dozen or more paintings in specially built racks for holding the paintings to keep them from banging into each other. Probably half of the paintings were of this GG person. I also found a couple of note-books that I logged into evidence when I got back."

"What's in the notebooks? Did you check them out?" Stone asked.

"Not yet. I was kinda excited to get back and see what you found," Cross replied.

"Well, now that we know her name, hopefully, it will be easier to determine once and for all whether the woman in the emerald dress is actually Gabriella Gibson," Stone replied.

"Yeah, not to mention what Michael Hawkins' murder has to do with all this," Cross added.

"Let's just hope that Gabriella Gibson is her real name and not a pseudonym," Stone retorted.

"I don't even want to think about that," Cross said.

"Well, there's one way to find out," Stone said as she turned around and started banging away on her keyboard. Cross held his breath while Stone did a quick Google search, sighed, and said, "There are results for her work but nothing much at all pertaining to who she actually is."

"That's not a good sign," Cross said disappointed.

Stone stared at the name on the screen and asked, "Who are you?"

"Also, what, if anything, does the art broker Michael Hawkins have to do with it?" Cross asked.

As Stone started the process to request information through the DMV, she said, "I was thinking about that. I wonder if Hawkins knew who Gabriella Gibson really was, and someone broke into his house and forced it out of him?"

Cross was silent for a second, then said, "I guess it's possible. That explains the torture and why whoever it was took their time in Hawkins's home that night ... they needed to find out who and where she was."

Stone said somberly, "He was protecting her ..."

"Yeah, if the woman in the emerald dress is indeed Gibson, they still found her," Cross said.

"That brings us to another problem," Stone said.

"Yeah ... we still have no clue who or why someone was after her in the first place," Cross said.

"Precisely," Stone agreed.

"So, what's our next move?" Cross asked.

Stone sat there deep in thought, then said, "What was the name of that yacht on the first painting we found hidden in the office?"

"*Omertà*," Cross said, "Why?"

"Somehow, I believe that painting is the key to everything. That painting was hidden for a reason. If we can find out anything about that yacht, it may lead us ... somewhere." Stone suggested.

"Okay then, why don't I go to evidence and see about getting copies of the notebooks I brought earlier? Maybe they can tell us something," Cross said.

"And while you do that ... I'll call someone I know in the FBI to see if they can help me track down the name of this yacht," Stone replied.

Cross rolled his eyes and groaned, "Not Davenport again..."

"Yes, Davenport," Stone replied. Don't worry, though. He's not even in the state; he's still in some sort of training in Washington. I'm going to give him a call. He has access to certain databases that we don't."

"Yeah, but at what cost?" Cross grumbled as he got up to see if he could get copies of the notebooks he had brought in earlier.

Stone snickered at Cross and said playfully, "Get out of here."

As soon as Cross left, Stone took her cell phone out of her pocket and scrolled through her contacts list until she got to Davenport's name and hit the button. After a few rings, Stone heard Davenport's familiar voice, "Hi, beautiful! What's going on?"

"Hey, Davenport," Stone replied as she tried not to grin at what he said, "I need a favor."

"I'll help if I can, but you remember I'm still in D.C., right?" Davenport asked.

"Yeah, I remember, but I'm still hoping you can help me."

"Whatcha need?" Davenport asked.

"I am working on a case and need information on a yacht named the *Omertà*."

"I may be able to help you. Where was it based out of?" Davenport asked.

"I have no idea," Stone replied sheepishly.

"How big of a yacht are we talking about?"

"I ... uh ... don't know," Stone again replied.

"You're not exactly giving me a lot to work with here. Are you, Stone?"

"Look, I'm sorry, Davenport. All I know is this case surrounds a painting of a yacht named the *Omertà*. It was hidden in a dead man's office, which could indicate—"

"Someone was after the painting," Davenport replied.

"It's at the least very possible," Stone answered.

"Let me dig into it and see what I can find. You know this is going to cost you the next time I'm in town. Don't you?" Davenport asked.

"Yeah, yeah, I figured," Stone smirked as she hung up the phone.

Stone then checked with SLED to see if they had any information on the woman named Gabriella Gibson, whom they strongly suspected was the woman in the emerald dress but still could not be certain about.

After hanging up with SLED, Cross returned to their home-away-from-home with his patent broad smile and said, "I may have something."

"That's fantastic because I don't have squat," Stone admitted sadly, whatcha got?"

"It's not much, but it could prove useful," Cross said.

"Ok, spill it. What is it?" Stone prodded.

"I have an address. I have not looked it up yet, so I have no idea what's there. It could be a gas station, for all I know."

"And where did you get this address?" Stone asked.

"It was written on a slip of paper with the notebooks I brought back," Cross said.

"Well, I talked to Davenport, and he said he would let me know when he finds something, so let's take a look."

Cross showed Stone the address, and in a few minutes, she had the address pulled up on Google Maps. Zooming down to street view, Stone said, "It looks like it used to be an old store or something sitting off by itself. It's a little run-down but nothing bad. What's supposed to be there?"

Cross shrugged his shoulders and answered, "I have no idea. It was just the address and nothing more."

Sliding her chair back, Stone said, "Let's check it out."

"Sounds like a plan," Cross replied.

Not long after leaving the department, Stone's cell phone rang. Stone glanced at the name on the ID, which read SINGH.

Stone answered the phone and said, "Hi. Doctor Singh, I have you on speaker and Cross is here with me."

"Superb," Singh said, "I have some news about Mr. Hawkins's death. It would seem that he did, in fact, die from a heart attack. I did find heart medications in his system, so he was taking his medicine as he was supposed to be, but his heart simply could not withstand the stress."

"I'm sure because I haven't seen someone take a beating like that in a long time," Stone said, "anything else?"

"I'm afraid not. My assessment of his time of death was spot on, and I'm sticking to the original time of between ten o'clock and two o'clock in the morning."

"Thank you, doctor," Stone said. Before Singh hung up the phone, Stone added, "By the way, doctor, have you found anything else about the woman in the emerald dress who was found in the lake?"

"Nothing yet, but I have sent her DNA off to an outside lab to be profiled in hopes of finding a match somewhere. Why? Is there something significant that I should be aware of?"

"We don't have any proof yet, but we highly suspect that the woman in the emerald dress is an artist named Gabriella Gibson. We just can't prove it, and if that is indeed her, she has no identification or driver's license that we can find."

"I shall endeavor to help you in your quest to pull the veil of secrecy off the young lady," Singh said empathetically.

"We appreciate your help, Doctor Singh," Stone said.

"You are most welcome," Singh replied before simply hanging up the phone.

After getting off the phone with Singh, Stone and Cross sat silently for the next few minutes, each lost in their own thoughts about the case. Shortly, Stone pulled into a small parking lot of what once was an old store in the early 40s or 50s.

Stone and Cross got out and cautiously approached the front of the building. Looking around, Cross said, "We had buildings like these all over the place back home in Alabama. Most of them were family-run, general stores that couldn't compete with the bigger stores."

Before Stone could say anything, Cross stopped dead in his tracks. "What is it?" Stone whispered.

Cross pointed to the ground at two sets of footprints leading to the back of the old store without saying a word. Both Stone and Cross drew their service weapons, approached the side of the building, and carefully peered into the nearest window of the once grand old store.

After Stone looked inside, she whispered to Cross, "It looks like some sort of studio. This could be where the woman in the emerald dress, aka Gabriella Gibson, worked or stayed."

Cautiously, both walked around the side of the building as quietly as possible. When they got around back and closer to the door, they both heard movement inside.

Cross took a long, slow, deep breath and glanced in the door of the old building while presenting as small of a target as possible. After glancing inside, Cross looked over his shoulder at Stone and shook his head, indicating he had not seen anyone.

Using a series of hand signals, Cross indicated that on the count of three, he would cross over to the right side of the door while Stone should stick to the left. Stone nodded that she understood and watched intently as Cross held up one finger, then the second, and finally the third.

On the count of three, Cross burst through the door shouting, "Lexington County Sheriff's Department! Come out with your hands up!"

Stopping two steps inside and to the right of the door, Cross paused with his weapon at the ready, covering Stone. At the same time, she entered the building and immediately stepped left.

"We know somebody's in here!" Cross snapped, "It would be better for all involved if you just showed yourself and came out!"

Both heard movement in what appeared to be another room near the back of the building and cautiously moved toward the sounds. As Stone and Cross made their way through a large open room filled with old dusty furniture, a figure emerged from the room's entrance, where the sounds emanated from and opened fire.

The figure snapped off three rounds in rapid succession and then ducked back into the room. "Holy shit!" Stone shouted, "You good Cross?"

Cross, who had ducked behind a large piece of furniture, glanced at Stone and said, "All good! Cover and move! Cover and move!"

Before either one could react, the figure reemerged in the doorway just long enough to fire off two more rounds and duck back into the room. "What in the hell do you want to do?" Stone asked as she took her portable radio off her side and called for immediate assistance.

The next thing they knew, both heard the sound of breaking glass as one of the men apparently was breaking a window to try and escape. As Cross started to leave cover to advance on the doorway, the same figure stepped out of the doorway and prepared to fire at the advancing Cross.

Before he could, though, Stone let loose two rounds that plugged the figure square in the chest. The figure crumpled to the floor in a heap in the small hallway outside the room. Pausing for a split second, Stone stood and closed in on the now prone figure while Cross covered her. After checking for a pulse and not finding one, Stone shook her head at Cross, who was still keeping her covered from nearby. As Stone carefully moved the gun away from the dead figure, Cross left cover with his weapon still aimed at the doorway.

Now together again outside the door, both took a deep breath, and Cross yet again took the lead and led the charge into the room where the unknown occupant had been last heard. After both made entry into the smaller room, it was immediately evident that whoever the second person in the room was had escaped out of the window.

"Damn!" Cross snapped as he looked out the window to see if he could see anyone.

"What in the hell was that about?" Stone asked wild-eyed.

As Cross checked out the figure Stone had shot, he made eye contact with her and said, "I have no idea, but good shooting. Both shots hit nearly center mass."

Within moments, multiple sirens could be heard approaching from different directions as the cavalry started arriving. Before long, the entire area was filled with flashing lights as several officers secured the scene, and others looked for the individual who was still on the loose.

It wasn't long before Chief of Detectives Stephen Boone arrived on the scene. "Are you two all right, and what in the hell happened?"

"Aw, chief, you didn't have to come all the way down here just to check on us," Stone said with a smirk.

"I didn't do it just for you!" Boone snapped, "I always check on my detectives when something like this happens. You should know this by now."

"Yeah, yeah," Stone said, "Cross found this address in a notebook written by the deceased, Michael Hawkins. There was nothing else with it to tell us what was here. It was just the address, so—"

Boone interrupted, snapping, "So, you two cowboys decided to come and check it out on your own without backup or telling anyone where you were! Do you know how stupid that was?"

"Yes, chief, but honestly, we didn't think anything would happen. We—"

"Were stupid and almost got yourselves killed! That's what!" Boone snapped, "Anyway, I'm off my soapbox. What happened?"

"It's like Stone said. We just came to see what was here and found the back door open. We made entry and came under fire from this guy," Cross said as he pointed at the figure on the floor in the doorway. When we entered the room, his partner escaped through the window."

"So, what does this address or the person you just shot have to do with the case?" Boone asked.

"Honestly, we have no idea yet," Stone said, "We haven't had much chance to investigate the area."

"Well, the shooting team is on the way to go over what happened. I gotta confiscate both of your weapons for now. You are also entitled to talk to your union reps. You guys know the drill. You gotta go to the hospital for a drug and alcohol test. Then you have a shit-ton of paperwork to take care of when you get back to the department," Boone replied, "and I'm going to want the paperwork done before your end of tour today. Try not to worry about it, though. It seems pretty cut and dry. You guys came under fire. You returned fire, killing one of the suspects—end of story. And don't worry about this place. I will ensure it's under lock and key until you two can return to look around."

"Yes, boss," they both replied somberly.

The rest of that day and well into the night were spent reviewing the events of that day and what happened when Stone and Cross got to the property in question with the shooting team.

After finally being allowed to leave, Stone and Cross walked out to their respective cars, and Stone asked, "You wanna grab a beer?"

"Are we okay to, after what happened today?" Cross asked.

"Sure, we are. We just can't talk about what happened today," Stone said.

"Believe me, the last thing I want to talk about is what happened today," Cross replied.

"You wanna go to the usual place?" Stone asked.

"Sounds good," Cross replied, "I'll follow you over."

∾

TWENTY MINUTES LATER, Stone and Cross walked into their familiar after-work hangout and grabbed two seats at the bar. The bartender approached them, and before he could even ask, Stone said, "I'll have whatever's on tap."

"Same for me," Cross said with a tired and forced smile.

"Coming right up," the bartender snapped.

Cross waited for the bartender to get out of earshot, then leaned in and asked, "What in the hell do you think is going on here?"

Stone took a deep breath and replied, "I am not sure, but the pieces are starting to fall into place."

"How so?"

"Well, look at it like this: We know Michael Hawkins was tortured for some time, his home office was broken into, then his second office was broken into and ransacked. When we got there, we found what?"

"The hidden painting," Cross replied.

"Exactly. And the hidden painting happens to have the same initials as the sketch pad, which was supposedly owned by the woman we fished out of Lake Murray."

"So, what you think is somebody was trying to find Gabriella Gibson, apparently to kill her. Whoever wanted her dead couldn't find her and tortured Hawkins to get to her."

Before Stone could reply, the bartender returned with their beers, then turned and walked off. Stone picked up her beer, took a big gulp, and replied, "Well, it's a theory. I have no idea who wanted her dead or why, but for now ... it's all we have."

Cross replied, "Tomorrow, we need to go back to that address and look around."

"I agree," Stone said, "but enough talk about today. Drink your beer."

7

The next morning, Stone and Cross met back in their cubicle, and as soon as Cross walked in, he said, "Morning. I was thinking about something last night."

"Oh, and what's that?" Stone asked.

"There are two things I don't understand," Cross said, "If the painting was the key to everything, why didn't he put it in his vault where he *knew* it was going to be safe?"

"I have no idea," Stone said, "what's the other thing?"

"I found the address on a piece of paper in Hawkins' storage unit. With that being said ... how in the hell did those two beat us there?"

"Well, right off hand, I would say, Hawkins told them to keep whoever broke into his home from killing him and possibly buying himself time to warn GG. As for the first part about hiding the painting instead of putting it in his self-storage unit ... I'm not sure."

When Cross didn't say anything, Stone looked at him and could tell he was deep in thought about something, "What's going on in that brain of yours?"

"Okay, well, riddle me this then, Batman.... How did somebody know when to be on the *Spirit of Lake Murray* to kill who we think is GG?"

"That's a damn good question," Stone replied, "I got nothing right now. If Singh can identify the guy I popped yesterday, that will lead us somewhere."

"Well, let's go back to that address where we got jumped. We'll take a look around, then call Singh and see if he's got anything on our dead guy from yesterday. Sound good?"

"Sounds fine to me," Cross replied. "Let's go talk to Boone and see what he thinks."

Stone and Cross knocked on Chief of Detectives Boone's office. "Enter," came the muffled reply from inside.

Stone and Cross walked in and closed the door behind them as they entered. "Oh, shit. This can't be good," Boone said as he looked at them.

"Now, why would you say that, boss?" Stone asked innocently.

"Because I have a sneaky suspicion that I already know what you want. You know you can't go out in the field without weapons, and although the shooting was cut and dry, you have not been cleared yet," Boone replied.

Stone held her hands out with her palms upward and pleaded, "Come on, Boss. We're essentially working a double homicide here."

Boone took a deep breath and said, "I can't get your weapons back this early ... and you both know I'm not supposed to let you two go back out in the field yet, especially unarmed, so here's what I'm going to do. I am going to allow you two to return to the store where the shooting occurred ... BUT and this is a huge but ... but two deputies will meet you there, and they will remain there while you have a look around. Once you're done looking around, you two will have to get your asses back here ASAP before one of my bosses finds out what's going on because if you two get caught out there, it's my ass on the chopping block. Now do what you gotta do and get back here."

THIRTY MINUTES LATER, Cross, Stone, and two Lexington County Sheriff's Deputies were pulling up to the building at the same address where they had been shot at just the day before. Looking at the two deputies, Stone said, "You guys take a quick walk around the perimeter of the building. We will post up here and wait for you to come back. Then we all go in together."

One of the deputies, a sergeant with massive, tattooed forearms, shook his head and said, "Sorry, no can do. I have orders to go in first and clear the place before you come in."

"Oh, you do. Do you?" Stone said with a huff.

"Yes, ma'am. I do, and I'm not about to let two unarmed detectives get shot on my watch," the sergeant said with a wink, "it would look bad on my resumé."

Stone smiled and replied, "Yes, sergeant. It would."

The four cautiously approached the building and, this time, took note of everything they saw. They stacked up against the back of the building, with Stone and Cross on one side of the door and the other two deputies on the other. The sergeant said, "We'll swing around the building and be right back ... do NOT move until I get back. Understand, detectives?"

Stone, in turn, held up her right hand with her index and middle finger extended upward and said, "Scout's honor. I promise. I won't go inside, sergeant ... what's your name anyway?"

"Sergeant Luke Marshall, ma'am,"

"Don't call me ma'am," Stone snapped sternly.

Marshall shook his head and said, "Sorry, that won't happen. I was raised in the South and became a man in the USMC. I only fear two people on this planet, my mama and my drill instructor, and you're neither one, so ma'am, it is."

Stone stared at Marshall momentarily, then she cracked a small smile and said, "I can appreciate that. Well, why don't you and your deputy take a stroll around the building and come back."

Marshall winked and said, "Yes, ma'am," before slinking around the corner of the building with the other deputy.

No sooner had Sergeant Marshall and the other deputy disappeared around the corner than Stone squared up to the door and placed a well-aimed kick beside the door handle. As the door flung open, Stone looked at Cross and said, "See, you're not the only one who can kick in doors."

"And just what in the hell are you doing?" Cross snapped.

"Going inside. What does it look like?" Stone answered.

"You literally just told the sergeant that you were going to wait for him to come back. You know he's going to be pissed when he comes back around, and we're not here. Right?"

Stone smiled devilishly and said, "Yep. I know. Besides, there's no doubt he heard me kick the door in and is already heading back around here," as she cautiously entered the building.

Stone and Cross had hardly gotten five feet inside the building when from behind them, they both heard, "Damn it, detectives! What in the hell did I just tell you?"

"Relax, sergeant. The seal was still in place on the door, and the windows were frozen shut, so I knew nobody was in here."

"Still, though. You should have waited for me," Marshall snapped.

"Aw, was the big, strong Marine worried about me?" Stone prodded.

"No, ma'am, just about completing my mission without casualties," Marshall replied. "Now, stay put while Tompson and I look around first."

"Yes, sergeant," Stone said coyly as Cross looked warily at her. "What? He's cute," she whispered after Marshall and Deputy Tompson ventured deeper into the building.

Both deputies returned shortly, holstered their weapons, and said, "Okay, the place is empty. Now, you two can have a look around."

Stone glanced at Cross, then looked at Marshall, hit her chest with a fist, and replied in a caveman's voice, "Uug ... big, strong man ... say it ok for little woman to enter."

Ignoring Stone, Marshall looked at Cross and asked, "Is she always like this?"

"I'm afraid so, sergeant," Cross replied with a chuckle as Stone and Cross ventured deeper into the building.

Stone and Cross left Marshall and Tompson guarding the back door and walked around the larger room, carefully examining the surroundings as they went. Several paintings apparently completed and still drying, were sitting on easels in the larger space.

Upon examining the completed paintings, Stone looked in the bottom right corner and found the all too familiar initials GG. "It seems like this is definitely the studio of the infamous Gabriella Gibson," Stone said as she looked around.

Cross replied, "Yeah, if we're lucky enough, we will find something in here, like a picture of Gabriella Gibson, and if we do, whatcha wanna bet that it's going to be a match for the woman in the emerald dress?"

"No bet," Stone replied as she left the main room and walked into an adjacent smaller room, "Gibson used this room as her living space," Stone called out to Cross, who was still in the main room.

Looking around the smaller room, Stone saw a cot in one corner and several tables with various items, such as a small portable refrigerator, microwave, and coffee maker.

As Cross joined Stone in the smaller room, he asked, "Have you found anything yet?"

"Not yet, but I just got started," Stone replied as she knelt and looked under the cot. Not finding anything under the cot, Stone then picked up the flimsy mattress of the frame and looked underneath to find nothing there as well.

Once she dropped the mattress and stood up, Stone put her hands on her hips and did a slow 360°-degree turn, taking in the entire space, "Where would I hide something?" Stone said aloud.

"What are you thinking?" Cross asked.

Stone shrugged her shoulders and said, "I have no idea, but there has to be something here. I can feel it. Why ... why would somebody go through all this trouble to find and kill an artist that by all accounts is a recluse?"

"I don't know, but we have to be figuring this out, or Boone is going to kill us," Cross replied as he joined the search and started looking around the small room.

They searched the room for another twenty minutes without

finding anything useful. After deciding to go back into the studio and search there again, Cross spotted something in the corner.

"Get a look at this," Cross said.

"It's a stack of old boxes ..." Stone countered.

Cross replied, "Exactly, but do you see anything different?"

Stone examined the boxes momentarily, then snapped her fingers and said, "I do now! There's no dust on them. Most everything else is covered in dust around here, but not those boxes, which means they haven't been there that long."

"Give the lady a cookie," Cross replied with a smile.

"Let's take a look and see what we have. Shall we?" Stone said as they walked over to take a closer look. "You wanna do the honors since you noticed it?"

"Sure," Cross said with a smile.

Cross took off the first two boxes, which were empty, and set them aside, but the third had weight, meaning there was absolutely something inside. Cross took his flashlight off his belt, opened the box's top flaps, and shined his light inside.

"Whatcha got?" Stone asked as Cross looked in the box like a kid opening a present on Christmas morning.

"I have a bunch of stuff, including—"

"What is it?" Stone asked.

"Hello there. What have we here?" Cross said as he pulled a hefty handheld device out of the box and moved into the light so they could examine it better.

As soon as Cross got it in the light, his eyes widened, and he said, "Well, I'll be damned."

Stone looked at the device, which had a boxy shape on top but a pistol-type grip, not unlike their service weapons. On one side was a small display along with several programming buttons. "This could be the break we have been looking for."

"What are you talking about?" Stone asked.

"This is a portable handheld barcode and QR code printer capable of printing on different surfaces ... including canvas," Cross replied.

"What does that mean for the case?" Stone asked, confused.

"I have no idea, but it must have meant something to her, which is why she hid it like she did. It may point us in the right direction if we can figure out what that is."

Stone asked, "Is there some sort of memory recall on there where we can see what the last thing she printed was?"

Stone watched briefly as Cross looked at the handheld device and said, "Maybe, but if there is, I can't find it."

"This thing might not even be relevant," Stone said, "for all we know, she prints barcodes on the back of her paintings for … authenticity or some shit."

Cross considered what she said and replied, "There's only one way to find out," before turning and abruptly walking out of the smaller room and into the studio area.

Stone followed him move for move and asked, "What are you thinking?"

Ignoring the question, Cross carefully took several of the finished paintings and turned them around, exposing the back of the canvas. Then he again took his trusty flashlight off his side and thoroughly examined the back of the painting, looking for any signs of a barcode or QR code. After looking over every square inch of the back of the canvas and not finding anything, Cross shook his head and said, "Damn! I thought I had something."

Stone thought for a moment and said, "Maybe you do. You're just looking in the wrong place!"

Stone turned the painting over and began methodically searching the entire canvas print but did not see a barcode or a QR code. "Well, that sucks, I thought maybe it was hidden in the painting itself."

Cross said, "I think you're on to something! There may be a QR code here, but we can't see it."

"So how do we find it?" Stone asked.

Cross took out his phone, turned his camera on, and, starting in the upper left corner, scanned the entire front of the woodlands painting with his camera. After scanning most of the painting, Cross thought his idea was not going to pan out, but suddenly, in a busy section of the painting where there were dense trees ... he struck paydirt.

"Well, well, well. Would ya look at that?" Cross said as he smiled at Stone. They both were slightly amazed when a nondescript web address appeared. Cross clicked on the address, and instead of a website, an audio file appeared.

"Holy shit!" Stone said excitedly, "Play it. Let's see what we have."

Cross hit the play button, and after a second, they heard the beginning of a conversation:

"So, Mr. Rhodes, welcome to the Omertà."

"What in the hell did we just listen to?" Cross asked.

"I have no idea, but we have a new name to look into now, that's for sure," Stone replied, "and that makes the second time the name of that damn yacht has come up now. Whatever it is, it's at the center of this case."

"You've got to be kidding me," Cross replied. "There's no way we can find information on this, Mr. Rhodes' character. We have no idea where to look."

"I know, but it's something..." Stone replied.

"You know what this means now, don't you?" Cross asked.

"Yep, it means we have to find every painting we can of Gabriella Gibson's and scan it to see if there are any more hidden files," Stone replied.

Stone's phone rang as they began to look at the other paintings in the studio. Looking at the caller ID, Stone said, "It's Singh. Hopefully, he has something on the woman in the emerald dress."

Stone answered the phone and put it on speaker so Cross could hear, "Hello, Dr. Singh. I have you on speaker with Cross. What do you have for us?"

"Good morning, detectives, although somehow I don't think you are going to be happy with what I am about to tell you," Singh replied.

"Oh, and what's that?"

"I still don't have anything on the young lady from Lake Murray as of yet, but I do have an identification on the person you shot yesterday."

"Well, that's something," Stone said, "who was he?"

"He was a man by the name of Fausto Tutino," Sing replied, "I found his fingerprints in the criminal database as a member of the Sorrentino crime syndicate."

"Oh, shit," Stone replied.

"Although I don't condone your choice of words, detective, I shared the sentiment when I first saw who he was connected to as well," Singh replied, "anyway, I felt you should know."

"Thank you, doctor. We appreciate the heads-up. Please let us know when you have something on the young woman."

"I will most assuredly do so," replied Singh.

"The boss is not going to be happy. This thing is spinning out of control," Cross replied.

"Yeah, as sad as this is to say, this is no simple double murder. There is something much deeper going on here," Stone replied.

"We gotta call the boss and get a full team here to inventory these paintings and make sure we don't miss anything. This is way too big of a job for just us," Cross said.

"Yep, this is not going to be fun," Stone said. "We have to check every single one of her paintings since we haven't found any list saying which paintings have hidden files."

"Maybe there's a list or some sort of inventory of paintings in those notebooks I brought back yesterday," Cross suggested, "I guess we should start by checking the paintings we have here and then seeing about tracking down other paintings that may have been distributed already."

"There almost has to be a list somewhere. In the meantime, we need to keep this place secure and make sure nothing happens to these paintings," Stone said.

Stone called Chief of Detectives Boone and filled him on what they had found, and even though they were not technically supposed to be there, Boone allowed them to stay and help out since they had been the ones that very well may have broken the case wide open.

While Stone talked to Boone, Cross walked over to the back door and informed Sergeant Marshall that they had found something important and were expecting a lot more people from the department to show up.

"Great," Marshall said, "how long are we gonna be stuck here?" He asked.

"As long as it takes," Cross replied, "as long as it takes."

Before long, a forensics team showed up at the old store-turned-studio and began the arduous task of separating all the paintings on the property and looking for anything else that could be hidden in the paintings or in the building.

After another two hours of searching, the team found two other files on different paintings with the exact same message. Cross and Stone told the forensics team they had to get back to the department to start digging into the recording and checking the notebooks Cross had found yesterday. They left word with the team lead that if another recording was found, they should be contacted immediately.

As Cross and Stone started to leave, they approached Sergeant Marshall at the back door and said, "We are heading back to the department now. We need to make sure this place is kept under lock and key until it is processed."

"That's going to be kind of hard to do, ma'am, since you didn't wait for me and kicked the door in," Marshall snapped. "What am I supposed to do with this busted lock?"

Stone shot an evil glance at Cross, then looked at Marshall and said, "You were a Marine—"

Marshall interrupted her mid-sentence, saying, "Once a Marine, always a Marine, ma'am!"

"Okay then, well, adapt and overcome," Stone said coyly.

Marshall smiled devilishly and said, "Ooh-rah, ma'am."

8

As Cross and Stone went back to their vehicle, Stone glanced at Cross and could tell he was thinking about something, "What's on your mind?"

"Just the fact that we came here looking for clues to whether or not the woman in the emerald dress was indeed Gabriella Gibson or not, which we never did do, by the way, and ended up finding out this case is much more complex than we had originally thought."

"Sometimes, that's how these cases work. We have to go where the leads take us," Stone replied, "but don't worry about the identification. A lot of the time, along the way, we find something else about the case that helps fill in what we don't know."

"Which brings me to another question," Cross replied, "what or who rather is the Sorrentino crime syndicate?"

"I've heard of them, but I'm not too familiar with them myself," Stone admitted."

"Well, we need to dig deeper into this because it's killing me not being able to positively identify the woman we pulled from the lake."

"I know it is, but the answer's there. We just have to find it. Not only that, we have to find the people responsible for killing them both. However, I'm pretty positive one is already in the morgue," Stone replied.

"Yeah, I figured as well. I wonder ..." Cross said as his voice trailed off.

"What is it?" Stone asked.

"I wonder if we can't find anything about this reclusive artist because she is in witness protection," Cross asked.

"Believe me, I have thought about that as well, but you know how those guys are. If that is the case, we are screwed because they are not going to say either way. The witness protection program is just about as tight-lipped as they come."

"It's a good thing you know somebody in the FBI," Cross said with a smirk.

"Yeah, but the problem is that the Witness Security Program is not under the FBI; it falls under the U.S. Marshals Service, and they don't play nice with other government agencies," Stone replied.

"True," Cross replied, "hopefully, Davenport can give us something on the Sorrentino crime syndicate."

"When we get back to the bullpen, I'll give him a call. I need to talk to him anyway to see if he found anything on the name of the yacht *Omertà*."

"Speaking of the *Omertà*," Cross said, "I was thinking about something. We need to check the painting of the yacht we found and see if there is a hidden file in that painting as well. Who knows? That may be the reason it was hidden. Maybe that particular painting is the key we have been looking for."

"That is an excellent idea. I had also been wondering why that painting was hidden. Maybe now we'll know. I think you should probably do that first before checking out the notebooks. Whatcha think?"

"Sounds like a plan to me," Cross replied.

As Cross and Stone parted ways, Stone walked through the bullpen to the cubicle she and Cross shared. Stone collapsed in her chair for a minute before picking up her cell and scrolling through her contacts list until she saw Davenport's name.

Stone clicked on his name, which was immediately replaced with a picture of a handsome man, instinctively bringing a smile to her face. The phone rang a few times before she heard Davenport's cheerful self say, "Hey, beautiful. Sorry I haven't gotten back to you yet. I've been busy with this training."

"No problem," Stone replied. "Have you had a chance to do a little digging for me? If not, it's okay because I have found a little more information that goes along with what I asked about."

Davenport took a swig of a drink and replied, "Oh, really now. What have you found?"

"Not much, I'm afraid, but I have a few more blanks filled in," Stone replied. "Cross and I found a hidden sound file barcoded on one of the paintings. It was only one sentence, but it was of an unknown voice welcoming a man named Mr. Rhodes to the Omertà." After a brief pause, Stone continued, "There is more, but I'm not sure you wanna know the rest."

"Of course, I want to know the rest—wait, did you say Rhodes?"

"Yes, I did. Why?" Stone asked.

"Nothing..." Davenport replied as his voice trailed off.

"Bullshit, nothing!" Stone snapped. Now, what is it?"

"I can't say," Davenport replied sternly.

"What in the hell do you mean you can't say?" Stone nearly shouted.

Davenport replied calmly, "I can't because it's classified."

"CLASSIFIED!" Stone shouted. "If I could, I would reach through this phone and choke the shit out of you!"

"Amy, calm down. You know, there are certain things that I cannot talk about, and this is one of them. I cannot talk about it." Davenport replied again sternly.

"How the hell can this be classified? Unless ... unless part of this case is still active somehow..." Stone said as her voice trailed off.

Davenport took a deep breath and said, "Look, all I can say is that you are treading on ice thinner than a sheet of paper. After poking around a little, I got my hand slapped by the higher-ups telling me to stay out of it, which means there is something still going on. My guess is they have someone inside the syndicate's organization they don't want to be exposed, but that's only a guess."

An uneasy silence came over the call as Davenport tried to avoid the awkwardness of the question, "What is it? What aren't you telling me?"

"Before I tell you what happened and you start to freak out ... I'm fine—"

"What do you mean you're fine? What happened?" Davenport asked concerned.

"Cross and I went to check out an address yesterday that came up in the investigation. While we were there, we were ambushed and shot at by two men. One got away, but I put two rounds in the chest of one of the guys," Stone paused a minute and said somberly, "he didn't make it."

"My God! That's terrible, Amy. What about Cross?"

"Yeah, he's fine. Neither of us were hurt."

"Who was the guy you ..."

"Shot? It's okay, you can say it," Stone replied.

"So, who was he?" Davenport asked as he tried to side-step the fact that the woman who was once about to be his fiancé just killed somebody.

"His name was Fausto Tutino. He had a long rap sheet and had ties to the syndicate. He was probably an enforcer or low-level hitman."

"I'm not so sure about that," Davenport replied.

"Why?" Stone asked concerned.

Davenport said, "Put it like this, if the syndicate needed to keep something from getting out, they would send some pretty bad boys to ensure success. They would not send a couple of low-level street thugs across the country. They would send some of their best."

After a pause, Stone said, "That means there is still at least one at large ... possibly more then."

"Great, just great," Davenport huffed. "That actually does go along with what I've found, and I have to say it's not good."

"Do I wanna know?" Stone groaned.

"No, but it's something you *need* to know," Davenport replied.

Davenport heard Stone take a breath on the phone, then she replied, "Okay, lay it on me."

Davenport said, "The Sorrentino crime syndicate is a big outfit on the west coast. They're based in the Long Beach area of California, but they have a lot of territory that runs all the way from the coast to parts of Vegas and down to Phoenix."

"Okay, so they're a big deal out west. Why are they here?" Stone asked.

"I have no idea," Davenport replied. "But get this ... the head of the Sorrentino family owns a yacht, and you get one guess as to the yacht's name."

There was a moment of total silence on the phone as Stone digested what Davenport was saying. Then suddenly, Stone said, "That means the *Omertà* is right at the very center of this whole thing."

"Not only that, but it also means if the syndicate sent people out to South Carolina, which they apparently did ... it means they went to a lot of trouble for some reason."

"So, what you're telling me is they are worried about something, and whatcha wanna bet it has everything to do with the hidden sound files in those paintings?"

"No bet," Davenport said, "look beautiful. I am finishing my lunch break, but I have to get back to the class. You and Cross, keep your heads on a swivel and let me know if I can help. I'll do what I can."

"Thanks, Peter," Stone replied before hanging up.

Stone sat at her desk for the next few minutes, writing notes on what she and Davenport had discussed. After writing her notes, Stone sat back in her chair, propped her feet up on her desk for a while, and stared into space, thinking about the case.

Before long, Cross returned from checking out the painting they had found hidden under Michael Hawkins's desk. As soon as Stone saw Cross, she knew he had found something. "You are not going to believe this shit!" Cross said wild-eyed.

"What did you find?" Stone asked, her curiosity piqued.

"I found not one but *two* barcoded files!" Cross said excitedly.

"What do you mean two files?" Stone asked.

"Yeah, so the other files we found welcoming the mysterious Mr. Rhodes to the *Omertà* were, in fact, pointing us to the hidden painting. I found this on the painting we have in the evidence room," Cross said as he pressed play on his phone. After a second, they heard the same voices in a slightly longer conversation, along with the apparent background noises of a dinner table:

"So, Mr. Rhodes, are you enjoying your evening?"

"Um ... yes, although I must say I'm not quite sure how I got an invite to such an exclusive dinner."

"It has come to my attention that your security business is ... how shall I put this ... making a name for itself in the area, and I want to employ you."

"Employ me, how exactly?"

"I want your security firm to protect my ...business. In turn, I shall reciprocate."

"What in the hell?" Stone asked.

"Yeah, tell me about it. It sounds like a proposed deal or merger, maybe?" Cross suggested.

Stone tilted her head and said, "Either that or a subtle ... you're going to work for me or else..."

"I can see that too," Cross replied.

"So, what was the other file?" Stone asked curiously.

"It was an automated voice that simply said, Columbia Museum of Art," Cross replied.

"Great, just great," Stone replied, "looks like we're going on a field trip."

STONE AND CROSS entered the Columbia Museum of Art less than an hour later and asked to speak to the curator. After a moment or two of waiting, an older woman walked up, smiled pleasantly, and said, "My name is Evelyn Harper. How can I help you detectives?"

"Is there somewhere we can be a little more discreet?" Cross asked. We would rather not talk about police business out in the open."

"Yes, of course," Harper replied, "follow me to my office."

Stone and Cross followed Harper around the corner and down a side hallway to several offices, one of which read—Evelyn Harper, Chief Curator.

Closing the door behind them, Evelyn gestured for them to have a seat and asked, "So, what can I do for you two detectives?"

"That's actually a tough one," Stone said, "we're working on a case that has brought us here, and we're hoping you can help us."

"I'll do what I can. What do you need to know?"

Cross replied, "Without giving out too many details, we are wondering if you have ever heard of a local artist named Gabriella Gibson who signs her work with just the letters GG."

"Oh, my yes, although she's a bit of a mystery," Harper replied.

"How so?" Cross asked.

"She is an up-and-coming artist for sure, so we were ecstatic when she reached out to us to see if she could donate one of her newest paintings."

Cross and Stone glanced at each other and could hardly contain their selves when they heard Harper talk about her donating a painting. "Tell me, Mrs. Harper, do you still have the painting?"

"Oh, my yes. We are required to hold on to the painting for a period of ten years."

"I see. And why is that?" Cross asked.

"It was what the artist wanted," Harper said.

"You wouldn't happen to have a photograph of the artist by any chance. Would you?" Stone asked.

Harper shook her head and said sadly, "I'm sorry, detectives, but no. That was one of the things she requested. Miss Gibson was a very private person and wanted to keep her identity as much of a secret as she could. At the dedication, she requested no photographs. May I ask what is happening and what this has to do with the art exhibits?"

"I'm sorry, but it's an ongoing case, and we can't discuss much. Can you show us the painting Gibson donated?"

"Yes, of course, right this way," Harper said as she got up, "if you will follow me, I will take you to it."

As everyone stood up and Harper ushered them out of her office, Cross said, "Just a moment. Is the painting on display?"

"Yes, actually, it is. Is there a problem?"

"We need to examine the painting in private. Can you arrange to take the painting to a back room where we can examine it out of the public eye?"

"Why in the world would you need me to do something like that?" Harper asked.

"Ma'am, this is not up for debate. We need to see the painting, please," Stone said sternly.

Harper's friendly demeanor disappeared as she looked perturbed at the detectives. "All right, if you must. I will see to it immediately. It will take about fifteen minutes. Please feel free to look around the museum. I'll find you as soon as it's been moved."

True to her word, fifteen minutes later, the curator appeared and took Cross and Stone back to a secure room where they examine the pieces before putting them out in public.

As they approached the painting, which was lying flat on a large table, Harper said sternly, "Please do not touch the painting. If it needs to be picked up or moved, I shall do it for you."

"Thank you, but that shouldn't be necessary," Cross said as he leaned over the painting. Cross looked at the painting in its entirety, a heavily wooded lakefront picture gently sloping down toward the water, where the dark greens and browns of the forest gave way to the orange hue of the clay near the water's edge.

"What are you looking for?" Harper asked as she closely watched the two detectives examine the painting.

"Ma'am, please stand back and give us some room," Stone said as she ushered Harper back a couple of feet so she couldn't see what they were doing.

Stone watched as Cross took out his phone and methodically

started scanning the painting, looking for the telltale signs of a barcode hidden within. Not long after the search began, Cross flashed his patented smile and showed off his nearly perfect teeth, and Stone knew he had found something.

"What do you have?" Stone asked Cross quietly as she glanced over her shoulder, ensuring the curator stayed out of the way.

"I found another barcode," Cross replied softly.

"What does it say this time?" Stone asked.

Cross listened closely and heard the same automated voice recording he had heard previously, which said, "Columbia Metropolitan Airport."

"The airport?" Stone asked.

"That's what it says," Cross replied.

"Well, I guess that's the next stop," Stone groaned.

9

Long Beach, California

Two thousand miles away, Lorenzo "Lenny" Sorrentino, the head of the Sorrentino crime syndicate, was sitting outside by the pool on his Long Beach estate, eating lunch with his grandchildren.

While he and his two grandchildren ate sandwiches and fresh fruits, several armed men walked the perimeter of the estate, looking for intruders or any indication that something could be about to happen. The Sorrentino family was strong, but they still had enemies.

"Do you like your sandwiches?" Sorrentino asked his two grandchildren, Olivia and Franca. The twins, both six years old, smiled, showing nearly identical toothless grins.

"Yes, Nonno," both replied lovingly as they munched on their sandwiches.

"You two are the cutest, toothless mice I believe I've ever seen," Sorrentino said, grinning as he lovingly rubbed their heads.

"We're not mice, Nonno," Olivia said, "we're your grandchildren, silly."

"You are?" Sorrentino asked, surprised as if it was the first time he had heard that.

"Yes, silly Nonno," Franca giggled.

Sorrentino looked up across the pool when he heard a nearby door opening. He shook his head when he saw Gianna, his daughter, and Vincent Marino, one of his top lieutenants, coming outside to talk to him.

"Boss, I have an update," Marino said.

"Just a minute," Sorrentino said, smiling at the children.

Sorrentino bent down, kissed his grandchildren on the top of their heads, looked at his daughter, and said, "Gianna, honey, will you take the children back inside while I have a word with Vincent."

Gianna knew more about the family business than most since she managed the legitimate companies and ensured the syndicate's public image remained untarnished, but not here and not now. Now, she was a mother.

Gianna ushered the children inside while Sorrentino watched and waited for them to get out of earshot. As soon as the three were inside, Sorrentino turned and glared at Marino, saying, "Didn't I tell you to never, never interrupt time with my grandkids."

"I'm ... I'm sorry, boss, but you said you wanted to be informed when we found something out."

"You're right, as usual, my old friend. What do you know?"

"Our man has reached out, and it's not good."

"Explain," Sorrentino said.

Marino took a deep breath and replied, "One of our men was killed in a shootout with the police. However, they did manage to silence the girl ... for good."

"What's the bad news then?" Sorrentino asked.

"Once they found the art dealer, it was only a matter of time before he talked," Vincent said with an evil snicker.

"So, it's taken care of then?" Sorrentino asked as he lit a large cigar.

"...Not exactly," Vincent confessed.

Sorrentino finished lighting the cigar, dropped the torch lighter on the table, and said, "And what do you mean by that?"

"After finding out where the broad stayed and taking her out of the picture, the boys went to her place to recover the recording. That's when they got jumped by the cops, and one of them was killed."

Sorrentino asked, "The one that's left ... who is it? Anybody we know?"

"Yeah, boss, it's Sisto Ciani."

"Isn't that the guy that helped us out of the jam a few months ago in San Diego?"

"That's the one boss," Vincent replied.

"Send word to him that if he succeeds in retrieving the recording, he will be my newest lieutenant, and he will have four men of his choosing working under him."

"Yes, boss. Do you want me to send more guys as backup? They can be there in five hours if they take the jet."

Sorrentino paused, considering what Vincent had said, then looked up at him and replied, "Send them."

ON THE WAY to the Columbia Metropolitan Airport, Stone pulled through a drive-thru so they could grab an early lunch and eat on the way to the airport. Since Stone was driving, Cross unbagged the burgers, handing one to Stone while she drove. Stone took a big bite, smiled, and said, "My stomach's happy now."

Cross took a bite of his cheeseburger, wrinkled up his nose, and replied sarcastically, "I don't see how. This stuff's nasty. It's barely edible."

"You eat cheeseburgers at Creekside," Stone reminded him.

"Yeah, but those are good, high-quality burgers. This is nothing more than processed garbage."

Stone smiled and replied, "There's the weightlifting geek I always knew was in there!"

Cross glanced at Stone and replied, "No, not geeking out on you, it's nutrition 101. Don't eat shit."

"Yeah, yeah," Stone said as she tore into her cheeseburger.

Twenty minutes later, Stone and Cross drove onto the property of the Columbia Metropolitan Airport and pulled to a stop near the sidewalk near an airport police vehicle. Both detectives walked inside and found their way to the information desk in the airport's atrium.

"Can I help you?" A woman working with the USO asked the detectives as she eyed their badges and guns.

"Yes. Is there a way you can get someone from airport police for us?" Stone asked.

"Sure, I can do that for you, just a moment," the woman said with a warm smile as she picked up the phone and told someone on the other end that two detectives were there and wanted to speak to someone in the Department of Public Safety.

While they waited, Stone and Cross looked around at the vast open atrium. "This place is huge," Cross said as he looked around the atrium.

"If you think this place is big, you should see Atlanta's airport," Stone shot back.

"Pass," Cross replied, as Stone laughed at his reaction.

Shortly thereafter, they both noticed a member of the airport police walking in their direction. As the man walked up, Stone noticed he had very short-cropped hair, glasses, and a short and well-groomed beard.

"Detectives, I'm Officer Sam King with the Department of Public Safety. What can I do for you?"

After shaking hands with the officer, Cross replied, "We are working on a case and need some information."

"What can I do," King asked.

"Do you have an art exhibit here in the airport?"

"We do. It's in the connector on the other side of security."

"We need to look at that exhibit. There are some paintings by a particular artist we are looking for, " Cross replied.

"That's not going to be a problem," King said, "I can escort you back, but I will have to stay with you."

"That's not a problem," Stone replied.

The three walked up to the side of the TSA security checkpoint, where flight crew usually enter. As King walked up, a young woman walked out from around a desk and said, "Hey, Sam. What are you up to?"

"Hey, Carly, I will be escorting these two detectives up the connector for a little bit."

"Not a problem," the short Latina replied.

The three walked through the side gate and around the security checkpoint lines. As they made their way through the bustling checkpoint, which was full of passengers trying to navigate the security screening process, Cross said, "Is it always this busy in here?"

"Not always. It comes and goes," King replied as they walked through the back of the TSA security checkpoint and started up the long connector toward the gate area, although they stopped just behind it.

"The artwork we have is hanging up here on your right and left and goes up the connector toward the gate area," King said as he pointed to the colorful paintings hanging on the walls between expansive windows that allowed passengers to see a nearly unobstructed view of several gates.

"I'll take the right, you take the left," Stone suggested.

"That sounds like a winner. I guess the first thing we need to do is see if we're in the right place. If we are and we happen to find a painting or two, then we can take our time and go over them with a fine-tooth comb," Cross replied as both started looking for paintings by the mysterious Gabriella Gibson.

In less than ten minutes, Stone and Cross each found a painting with the flowing initials of GG in the bottom corner.

"I found one," Cross called out from across the connector as passengers walked past, eyeing them both suspiciously.

"I have one over here, too," Stone replied as she took out her phone and began to methodically search the painting through her camera lens, hoping her camera would lock onto a QR code hidden within the painting.

Cross hovered his phone over a small section of the painting, and a small link appeared on his screen as he did. Once he tapped on the link, a small audio file began to play that only spoke one phrase in the same generic voice, "Lexington County Public Library."

"I got mine. What does yours say?" Cross asked.

Stone walked over and said, "Not here. I'll tell you in the car."

"Deal," Cross replied as they walked over to where Officer King was standing nearby.

"We got what we came for, and we're ready to head out," Stone told the ever-vigilant King.

"Wait a minute," Cross said, "technically, the paintings are now evidence. Shouldn't we take them with us?"

Stone thought for a moment and said,"No. We'll leave them where they are for now. They're safe here."

"In that case, right this way," King said as he started to escort them back down the connector, past the TSA security checkpoint, and back into the expansive atrium.

Once they walked into the atrium and were out of the way, the three stopped, and King asked, "Do you need anything else?"

"No, we got what we came for. Thank you for your help," Cross and Stone said as they again shook hands with King before leaving.

Stone and Cross walked silently back to their car and got in without a word. As soon as the door closed, Cross clapped his hands and rubbed them briskly back and forth, saying, "Okay, what juicy stuff was on your recording?"

Stone took out her phone and tapped play. After a moment, they heard the same voices on the other recordings: "*And just how would you reciprocate?*" The man who had been identified earlier as Mr. Rhodes asked.

"*My men lack specific skills required to do their jobs effectively. In return, I understand you have a stash of weapons at your disposal. I could open up my supply lines to you...*"

"What in the hell was that?" Cross asked with a mixture of shock and confusion.

"It sounds like some sort of agreement or merger is taking place," Stone replied.

"Sure does," Cross said. "The question now is who, why, and when?"

"So, what was on the painting you checked?" Stone asked.

"It was a simple audio file with the same automated voice, and it just said, "Lexington County Public Library."

Stone's phone rang before they pulled away from the curb at the airport. "Damn," Stone said. "It's the boss ... not what we need right now."

"It could be about the shooting, though," Cross said hopefully.

Stone answered the phone with an evil smile and said, "Hey, boss. We're at the airport. We're chasing down a lead as we speak."

"What? What lead?" Boone snapped.

Stone glanced at Cross with a smirk, who shot her a death stare, knowing she was getting ready to do something. "Yeah, this lead came up last minute; we gotta catch a plane. We're heading to the gate now. We'll be back in a few days. Sorry, but we had to charge two tickets to Hawaii on the work card."

"WHAT IN THE FU—!"

"Relax, boss! I'm just messing with you!" Stone said, smiling from ear to ear as Cross reached across the front seat and smacked her on the shoulder wild-eyed.

"Not cool!" Boone snapped, "Get your butts back here right now!"

Stone started to protest, "Boss, we ha—"

"The only thing you have to do is get your butts back here on the double! Or do you not want your service weapons back?"

Dumbfounded, Stone said, "Um, yeah, of course, we want our service weapons back, but how ..."

"How did your amazing boss get you two off the hook so fast? Is that what you were about to ask?"

"Yeah, sure, let's go with that," Stone said with a smirk.

"I didn't. Your boyfriend did," Boone replied.

"I'm scared to ask, but what does he have to do with this?" Stone asked.

"Just get your asses back here on the double," Boone replied before hanging up the phone.

"Wonder what that meant?" Cross asked.

"I have no idea, but Davenport doesn't have that kind of pull, so something else is happening, that's for sure," Stone replied as she pulled away from the curb and drove in front of the airport terminal, heading back to the Sheriff's Department.

"No, probably not. And by the way, you have got to stop scaring the bejesus out of me!"

Stone simply grinned and said, "I don't know what you're talking about."

As Stone and Cross left the Columbia Metropolitan Airport property, they never realized there was a car following them, move for move ... watching ... waiting.

10

Approximately twenty minutes later, Cross and Stone pulled into the Lexington County Sheriff's Department's secure parking lot and got out. Cross stretched his massive arms over his head, and a long, drawn-out groan came out simultaneously.

"You feel better?" Stone asked with a chuckle.

"For the time being," Cross said, "I gotta hit the gym sometime, though. I keep getting stiff from sitting in the car so much."

"Let's go find out what in the hell is going on," Stone replied.

Both Stone and Cross walked inside and, after walking through a proverbial maze of cubicles in the bullpen, they emerged on the other side and knocked on Boone's door.

"Enter," came the muffled reply from the other side.

Stone opened the door, and both she and Cross walked in. "It's about time you two got here," Boone quipped as he opened a drawer on his desk. Boone and Cross watched closely as he pulled out their service weapons and handed them over to them.

"I don't understand," Cross said as he and Stone checked their weapons and put them on their respective sides. "I thought shooting investigations took weeks."

Boone looked at both somberly and said, "Usually, they do, but the stakes have changed."

"In what way?" Stone asked.

Boone took a deep breath and said, "Why didn't you tell me what was happening?"

"We did," Stone replied.

"Well, you forgot an important part, namely the Sorrentino crime family!" Boone snapped.

"We weren't entirely sure they had anything to do with it until recently," Cross replied.

"Yeah, how did you find out about them?" Stone asked.

Your boyfriend—"

Stone interrupted Boone mid-sentence, saying, "He's not my boyfriend, but go ahead."

"My apologies," Boone remarked before rephrasing his statement, "Your friend in the FBI called me earlier. Even though he's stuck in D.C. in some sort of training, he reached out to the FBI office in California."

"Do tell," Stone replied as she crossed her arms.

"Yeah, and it's not good. One of Davenport's contacts, who has intimate knowledge of the Sorrentino family, passed along an important bit of information."

"Which is what?" Cross asked.

"Three hours ago, a private jet owned by the Sorrentino family took off from an airport in California with two pilots and four passengers onboard. According to our friends at the FBI, the filed flight plan is bringing them ... right ... here," Boone replied.

"And that's why we're getting our weapons back," Stone said as heaviness began to fill her chest.

"That is precisely why. I have talked to the higher-ups, and they got the shooting team to ... expedite matters," Boone replied.

"What's the jets eta?" Stone asked.

"They took off a few hours ago, so technically, they could be here in as little as two hours," Boone replied.

"Knowing this, let's greet them at the airport when they land, simple," Cross replied.

"Won't work," Boone replied. "They can and probably will amend their flight plan and land elsewhere at the last minute for that reason."

"Yeah, they can land at several airports and drive here in under two more hours," Stone said.

"So, essentially, what you're telling me is we could have as little as two hours and as many as four or five hours before their backup arrives, and we can't stop them," Cross replied.

"Precisely," Stone said.

"So, what's the plan?" Boone inquired.

"We are going to follow the clues. Hopefully, they will lead us somewhere quickly, and we can get to the bottom of this," Stone replied. "If that's everything, we got to get digging on this, boss."

"Yeah, go on. Get out of here. Just don't shoot anybody else," Boone replied.

Stone smirked and said, "No promises," as she closed the door.

After leaving Boone's office, Stone and Cross walked to their cubicle, where both plopped down in their respective chairs. "I feel whole again," Cross said as he gently stroked the .40 caliber Glock on his hip.

"Tell me about it," Stone said, "I felt totally naked working out in the field without mine."

Cross grinned and said, "Somehow, I think the sergeant who went with us would have been okay with that."

"And yet you didn't get defensive with him?" Stone questioned.

"It's different. He's one of us," Cross said with a smirk.

"Yeah, okay," Stone said. "What did the file say again?"

"It just said Lexington County Public Library," Cross replied.

"Looks like that's our next stop," Stone replied as she stood back up, looked at Cross, and said, "Ya coming?"

"We just sat down," Cross grumbled as he stood back up.

"Yeah, well, you can rest when you're dead. Let's go solve a case," Stone said.

~

STONE AND CROSS pulled into the Lexington County Public Library, parked, and walked inside. As soon as they walked in, they approached a young woman with a name badge that read Kimmy and asked if they had any artwork around.

"Oh, yes. We do. We have several paintings done by local artists hanging on the walls. Is there one in particular you're looking for?"

"We're looking for anything done by the artist Gabriella Gibson. She signs her paintings with just her initials," Stone said.

"I know just the one you're talking about. If you follow me, I will gladly show it to you," Kimmy replied.

"Lead the way," Cross replied.

"So, you only have the one painting from her," Stone asked.

"Yep, just the one," Kimmy replied.

Cross asked, "Do you happen to know if there is a picture of Gabriella Gibson here ... possibly donating the painting."

"No, sorry, there's not one I know of," Kimmy replied.

"Of course not. That would be too easy," Cross said under his breath to Stone.

Stone and Cross followed the young lady to a section of the library with local interests. When they entered the local interests section, Kimmy pointed to a painting on the wall and said, "There it is. Is there anything else I can do for you?"

"No, thank you. That will be all," Cross said, smiling at the young lady."

"Well, I'll be near the front if you need anything. Don't hesitate to come get me."

"Thank you," Stone replied.

"Well, let's take a look and see what we have. Shall we?" Cross asked as they walked over to take a closer look at the painting.

"This woman sure loved Lake Murray, didn't she?" Stone asked.

"It would appear so," Cross replied.

Stone looked in the bottom right corner of the painting and

quickly recognized the script GG, which they now knew stood for Gabriella Gibson.

Cross took out his phone and scanned the painting, starting in the upper left corner and working his way across it. After making several passes, a link appeared on the phone's display. "Got it!" Cross said.

"Play it and see what it says," Stone replied.

Cross hit the play button, and they heard the same automated voice as before, which simply said in a monotoned voice, "Green Acres."

Stone and Cross looked at each other, and Stone first asked the question. "What in the hell is Green Acres?"

"Other than the TV show, I have no idea," Cross replied.

"Looks like we need to be finding out," Stone said. "Let's get back to the office and start digging."

"Ya know, Creekside is right down the road. I'm just saying," Cross suggested.

"Yeah, I had thought of that too, but we don't have the time right now. Especially with us being on a time schedule before Sorrentino's backup gets here."

"I guess you're right," Cross replied.

After returning to the Lexington County Sheriff's Department, Stone and Cross went to work looking up what Green Acres could mean. Once they returned to their shared cubicle, Stone slid up to the keyboard and did a quick Google search, which produced hundreds if not thousands of hits for the television show Green Acres in the mid-60s and early 70s, and all the actors and actresses who played on it.

Stone did fifteen minutes of research on the television show and concluded it had nothing to do with what was happening with the case. Not only that, but there were hundreds more hits on all sorts of businesses, from plant nurseries to schools.

"Well, that's a bust," Stone said.

"It's gotta mean something," Cross replied. "All of the places that have been named where paintings were hanging have been around here. So, with that being said, what does Green Acres have to do with Columbia or Lexington County?"

They both sat in silence for a few minutes until Stone said, "Let me try something."

Cross watched as she typed Green Acres and Lexington, South Carolina, into the Google search bar.

The new search yielded page after page of new results for Green Acres in the Columbia area. Yet again, after wasting precious minutes searching copious amounts of hits, neither Stone nor Cross found anything relevant to the case.

"Are you sure it said Green Acres?" Stone asked.

"Positive," Cross replied confidently as he replayed the recording again."

After turning the sound all the way up and replaying the recording several times in a row, Stone said, "There's no mistake. It definitely says, Green Acres. But why?"

"Let's walk over and talk to the boss," Cross suggested, "Maybe he can give us a little help."

"When all else fails, talk to the boss," Stone huffed, "let's go."

A few minutes later, Stone and Cross knocked on Boone's door for the second time in the past half hour. "Enter," Boone replied.

As soon as the door opened, Boone looked up from his computer and said, "Shit. Somehow, I knew it was going to be you two. Come on in. What's up?"

"We've hit a bit of a snag," Stone said sheepishly. "We were wondering if you could help."

"What kind of help are you two looking for?" Boone asked.

Cross and Stone spent the next ten minutes giving Boone the rundown on what they had found and the recording they were stuck on.

"Play the recording," Boone replied.

Everyone sat quietly while Cross played the two-word recording. "It absolutely says Green Acres," Boone replied, "The question is, what does it mean?"

"We have no idea. That's where we're stumped. We don't know where to go now." Stone replied.

"Think ... think," Boone said aloud. "Why does that sound so damn familiar?"

Suddenly, Boone snapped his fingers, pulled out his personal cell phone, and started scrolling. After finding the name he wanted, he hit the call button and waited for someone to pick it up.

"Hey, sweetie ... no, nothing's wrong, but I have to ask you a question. "Where did we go with the kids on the field trip where they talked about the place called Green Acres?"

Cross and Stone sat there patiently, watching Boone's mannerisms as he listened, trying to discern whether the outcome would be in their favor. Finally, when they saw Boone smile, they knew he had the answer.

"Okay, okay, I'll make sure I stop on the way home ... love you too, gotta go bye!" Boone said as he hung up his personal cell phone and slid it into his pocket.

Stone smirked, looked at Cross, and asked, "Did the Chief of Detectives really just call his wife for help on a case?"

"I believe he did," Cross replied with his patented broad smile.

"You want to know what I found or not?" Boone snapped.

"So, what did the wifey tell you?" Stone asked, rubbing it in that he had to call his wife for help.

"I knew I had heard it before, but I just couldn't remember where," Boone replied. "Anyway, Green Acres was once called the Lorick plantation home."

"So, where is this Green Acres, aka Lorick plantation, located?" Cross asked.

Boone replied, "The Lorick plantation no longer exists, but the home still stands today. It's now the Lake Murray Visitors Center."

Stone's eyes widened, "That makes perfect sense. I guess that's going to be our next stop."

"You two need to get going. If you haven't figured it out by now, you're in a race against time. You have got to get this thing figured out before Sorrentino's backup shows up."

"We're on it, boss," Cross said as he and Stone got up to leave Boone's office.

11

As they got into the car, Stone asked, "So, have you talked to Yasmin and set up a time for a date yet?"

"No, not yet," Cross said as they started pulling out of the department's secure parking lot.

"Why not?" Stone asked curiously.

"Just haven't had the time," Cross grumbled.

"I'm driving. You have the time right now, so take out your phone and call her," Stone said.

"I don't know ..."

"What don't you know? I saw how she was when you were around. She seemed to be interested in you," Stone prodded.

"Yeah, I think she is too. I'm just not sure if ..."

"If what?" Stone asked.

"I'm just not sure the timing is right," Cross said as his voice trailed off.

"When is there ever a right time to find someone? Stone replied. "Especially with our jobs."

"Yeah, I know, but ..."

"No buts, she already knows what the job is like because she is in a similar situation with her job."

"That's true," Cross said, perking up. "I think I'm gonna call her. Do you mind if I do it now before I lose my nerve?"

"Not at all. We have almost fifteen minutes before we get to the Lake Murray Visitor's Center."

Cross took a deep breath and dialed Yasmin. After a few rings, Stone heard Cross say, "Yasmin? This is Detective Cross. Is now a good time? I wanted to see if you would like to have dinner with me this weekend." Stone waited an agonizing minute while Yasmin was talking, but then Stone saw Cross's face light up, and she knew...

Finally, Cross replied, "Saturday at eight is perfect! See you then."

Cross hung up the phone and looked at Stone, smiling from ear to ear. "I knew she would go out with me," Cross said, grinning.

"Yeah, sure ya did, partner. That's why you were scared shitless to call her," Stone said, giggling.

AT ROUGHLY THE SAME TIME, Stone and Cross were leaving the Sheriff's Department, which was not far away; a private jet arrived ahead of schedule at the Columbia Metropolitan Airport. Four men, each dressed in slacks, a button-up shirt, and a suit jacket, walked off the plane and got into a four-door car arranged for them before landing.

The leader of the four men was Nico Aufiero. He had grown up in a life of crime and became a member of the Sorrentino organization several years ago. Known for being a heavy hitter, he quickly moved up in the organization and became known as one of its best fixers.

As Nico settled in the passenger's seat of the car, he pulled his cell phone out, turned his speaker on, and dialed. After a few rings, "They heard a heavily accented voice say, "Youse here?"

Immediately, Nico recognized the voice of Sisto Ciani, who he had worked with in the past. "We're here. We just landed. Where are you now?"

"I'm following dese two detectives now. I'm gunna share my location so youse can follow me. Get here as soon as you can."

With a few clicks, Nico's phone changed to a picture of a map with a blue pulsating dot. "You see me?" Sisto asked.

"I see youse. The boys and I are on the way. Keep a close eye on them, and we will be there as soon as we can," Nico said before hanging up with a click. Nico looked at the driver and said, "We gotta move."

~

As Stone drove across the Lake Murray Dam, she glanced over at Cross, who was still smiling from ear to ear. She checked her rearview mirror and asked, "So, what are the plans?"

"Nothing much. We're just going to get a bite to eat and spend a little time together. That's all." Cross said.

"Nothing wrong with that," Stone said.

"How much further is this place?" Cross asked.

"Not far. We're about a mile and a half away from it now," Stone replied as she glanced in her rearview mirror again.

"What's going on? That's the second time you've looked in the rearview mirror since we've been on the dam." Cross said, a hint of concern in his voice.

Stone shook her head and said, "It's probably nothing, but I saw a white car like that at the airport, and now there's another one."

Cross glanced over his shoulder and said, "White four-doors are a dime a dozen."

"True," Stone replied as she saw Cross instinctively feel for his service weapon.

Stone was caught at the stoplight coming off the dam at the corner of Bush River Road and North Lake Drive, but when she could, she turned left and drove a short distance until they saw the visitors center on the right housed in what was once a magnificent old home.

After parking in the Lake Murray Visitors Center's side parking lot, Stone and Cross walked up the ramp to the side entrance and walked in. As they entered, Stone and Cross saw a young woman with long brown hair who happened to be walking by stopped and said, "Hello, my name is Cameron. I'm the Special Events Manager. Can I help you with something?"

"Possibly," Stone replied, "We're detectives with the Lexington County Sheriff's Office. We're working on a case and hoping somebody here can point us in the right direction."

The young woman who had introduced herself as Cameron said, "Well, you're in luck. Our Director is standing at the desk right there, talking with the concierge. Come on, and I'll introduce you to them."

"Thank you, we'd appreciate it," Stone replied.

Cameron walked with the two detectives to the desk where two other ladies were having a conversation. "Excuse me, Miriam, but these two detectives need help."

"I'm not sure what we can do, but we'd be glad to help if we can," the woman who exudes Southern charm replied as she extended her hand to the two detectives. "I'm Miriam Atria, the President and CEO of Lake Murray Country, and this is my Concierge and Visitor Center Specialist, Joanie Hess. We'd be glad to help you if we could."

"Absolutely we would," Hess replied.

"What sort of help do you need exactly?" Miriam asked.

"We are working on a case involving a local artist named Gabriella Gibson, and we have been told that one or more of her paintings are here. Is this correct?" Stone asked.

"Absolutely. Would you like to see it?" Miriam inquired.

"Yes, please," Cross replied.

"Right this way," Miriam said as she and Joanie led the two detectives into the next room, which was their gift shop.

Cross said, "Wow, you have a lot of merchandise."

"Yes, we do! We are quite proud of our little gift store," Joanie beamed.

As they walked through to another attached room, Miriam pointed to a painting hanging on the wall and said, "There it is. We are quite proud of it."

Cross looked at the tag hanging off the frame, which read "NOT

FOR SALE. "Many have tried to buy the painting, I'm assuming," Cross said as he pointed to the sign.

"Oh, yes," Miriam replied, "But that is not going to be sold." Suddenly, her eyes widened in horror as a thought struck her, "You're not going to confiscate our painting, are you?"

"Oh, no, nothing of the sort," Cross reassured her, "but we need to look at it closer. Do you mind if I take it down for a few minutes?"

"Not at all, just please be careful with it." Joanie requested.

"I promise. I'll be careful," Cross replied as he carefully took the painting off the wall.

"Is there somewhere where I can lay this down flat?" Cross asked as he carefully held the painting.

"Yes, of course, follow me," Miriam said as she let Cross across a small hallway, past what was once the front door of the grand old home, and into another room.

Cross gently laid the painting down on a sofa, took out his phone, and began scanning the painting just as he and Stone had done with the others.

Less than five minutes later, Cross found a hidden QR code. This one was also only held two words—password: WD4OIN

"What in the hell..." Stone said.

"I have absolutely zero idea," Cross replied as he carefully replaced the painting where it belonged.

Stone and Cross thanked the ladies at the Lake Murray Visitors Center for their help and walked outside to their car. After getting in their car, Cross asked, "Okay, so we have to be getting near the end if we now have a password. The only problem now is we don't know what the password is for."

Stone was quiet as she pulled out of the parking space and headed toward the side street. After pulling out onto the side street, Stone finally spoke up and said, "Curious, in every other instance, we were sent to a specific location to find a clue to the next place, like a scavenger hunt."

"I'm with ya so far," Cross replied. "So where do we go from here?"

"I have no idea, but for the time being, we have a bigger problem," Stone said as she glanced in her rear-view mirror.

"Don't tell me," Cross replied.

"Yep, the same car is back," Stone said as she started across the dam.

"Whatcha wanna do?" Cross asked.

"I know just the thing," Stone said excitedly.

"Dare I ask what that entails?" Cross asked concerned.

"We are going to set a little trap for whoever is following us," Stone replied.

"And just how are we going to do that?"

"Easy, my friend," Stone said. "He doesn't know that we're on to him, so I'm going to lead him to a deserted place, and we will get a couple of marked units to cut off his escape."

"Okay, sounds easy enough, but where?" Cross asked as Stone turned left onto Corley Mill Road.

"I'm thinking," Stone said as she looked in her rear-view mirror to ensure the car was still tailing them.

"Gotta think of something. I gotta be able to get cars moving in this direction," Cross said.

Suddenly, Stone smiled and said, "It's perfect!"

"I'm already not liking the sound of this," Cross muttered.

"Oh hush, ya big baby," Stone said. "Get on the portable and tell dispatch to have two of the closest cars stage at the gas station where Rica Mex is on Corley Mill Road. Tell them to wait there and move on my order."

"What are you going to do?" Cross asked.

"We're going to turn left up ahead onto Hope Ferry Road, which dead ends at the Hope Ferry Boat Landing at the Saluda River. One way in and one way out," Stone said as she smiled devilishly.

Cross got on the portable radio and told dispatch the plan, who immediately sent two marked patrol cars to the gas station with orders to wait for Stone's go-ahead.

Stone slowed up just enough to ensure the car following them saw where they turned. After the turn, Stone went the speed limit down Hope Ferry Road towards the boat landing, ensuring the car following them also made the turn.

When Stone and Cross were most of the way to the boat landing from Corley Mill Road, Stone said, "Now! Call in the calvary."

Cross grabbed the portable and said, "ROLL TIDE! Come and get 'em, boys!"

"On the move!" Came the reply from an unknown yet familiar voice.

"You just had to say it. Didn't you," Stone said as the paved road gave way to a simple dirt road.

"Yep, sure did." Cross snickered.

Stone and Cross continued down the dirt road until it connected to a large square paved area near the boat landing. As soon as Stone pulled into the parking area, she turned left and swung the car around, pointing back toward the only road in or out. The last thing she did was back into the corner of the parking area opposite the road so the following car would have to pass them when they pulled into the parking lot.

While waiting for the vehicle to follow them into the parking lot, Stone and Cross checked their weapons in case they were necessary. In the distance, they could hear a car coming down the dirt road.

As soon as the car pulled into the parking lot, the driver must have realized it was a trap. He immediately made a tight U-turn and started to return to the dirt road, but Stone was faster.

When she saw what the driver was doing, she hammered the gas and sped across the parking lot to cut the driver off from the only road leading out.

Stone, however, misjudged how tight the lighter, more maneuverable car could turn, and for the moment, it was a drag race to see who would get to the road first. Within seconds, though, the police cruiser with its larger engine started to gain ground. When it looked like they would be able to keep the vehicle from escaping—everything changed.

12

When Stone and Cross thought they would manage to cut off the car that had been following them, another vehicle burst onto the scene with four men inside and skidded to a halt.

"Who the hell are these guys?" Cross asked.

"I hope it's not who I think it is!" Stone yelled as three of the men jumped out of the car and began firing at Stone's cruiser.

As rounds pinged off the front of the police cruiser, steam started bellowing from the wounded radiator of Stone's car. Stone immediately slammed on the brakes, threw the car into reverse, and stomped on the gas to get separation from the other vehicle. While she did this, Cross got on the portable and screamed, "We're taking fire from a second car! Where are you guys?"

Immediately, the reply came back over the radio, "Hang in there! We will be there in less than a minute!"

Stone and Cross immediately began returning fire, firing as best they could from the windows of their still-moving car. Stone slammed on the breaks once they had regained some distance from the now five-man strong group. After opening up the range a little more, Stone and Cross both got out, crouched behind the doors of their patrol car, and began to return accurate fire.

"I'm out! Reloading! Cross yelled as Stone kept up her rate of fire to cover Cross.

As soon as Cross could start returning fire, Stone's gun jammed. "DOUBLE FEED! Stone yelled to Cross, indicating her weapon was jammed and, for the moment, was useless.

The five men in both vehicles must have been able to tell from the decreased gunfire that one of the officers might have been either hit or out of ammo because the men started to fan out in an attempt to outflank the police cruiser.

At that exact moment, the two marked patrol cars burst onto the scene and skidded to a halt nearby. Upon seeing this, all the men raced back to their respective vehicles and tried to escape; however, with both deputies now blocking the only road out and armed with AR-15s, there was nowhere to run.

In a desperate attempt to escape, the vehicle being driven by the lone gunman who had been following them jumped into his car and attempted to shoot the gap between the two police cruisers. As soon as the gunman's car surged toward the two cruisers, both deputies opened fire with their AR-15s. Within seconds, the car's windshield was turned into a spiderweb of cracks and bullet holes. The driver jerked several times as rounds from the deputy's AR-15s struck home, turning the interior of the car into a macabre scene as blood splattered the car's interior and streaked the windows.

The car immediately slowed and started coasting as the driver's foot slid off the gas pedal. The vehicle drifted toward one of the sheriff's cars and came to a halt against the deputy's reinforced front bumper. From her vantage point, Stone watched as the car driven by the lone gunman abruptly slowed and ran into the front of the deputy's cruiser with a bang. It was then that Stone realized that one of the deputies who had come to their rescue was none other than Sergeant Marshall, the tattooed Marine.

After a moment of struggling, Stone was able to clear her jammed weapon, then she and Cross, along with the other two deputies with their long guns, immediately turned their attention to the remaining car and its four occupants. For a fleeting moment, there was a proverbial Mexican standoff, but quickly enough, the armed men threw down their weapons and surrendered after seeing what had just happened to their comrade.

The two deputies armed with the AR-15s kept the four men covered while Stone and Cross quickly approached, handcuffing two of the men while the two deputies with the long guns approached the other two suspects with weapons at the ready.

Within minutes, all four surviving suspects were in custody, and the situation was under control. In the distance, sirens could be heard racing to the area from multiple directions. Sergeant Marshall got on the radio and announced that the situation was under control and that the responding officers could slow down.

The situation now under control, Marshall walked over to check on the two detectives, namely Stone, and asked, "You good?"

"Yeah, all good," Stone said as Marshall eyed Stone.

"I'm fine too. Thanks for asking," Cross remarked as he rolled his eyes at Marshall.

"I was getting to you," Marshall said. "But ladies first."

"Yeah, yeah," Cross replied. "I'm going over to check on the driver who tried to escape."

Just then, several more Lexington County Sheriff's deputies roared into the parking lot, swarmed the area, and started getting the handcuffed men up off the ground and into the back of their squad cars.

Stone looked at Marshall as Cross walked off and said, "Thanks for the assist. The guy you shot had been following us all day. No doubt he was waiting for his backup to arrive. We knew they were coming but didn't think they were this close."

Marshall smiled and replied, "Yet another win for the US Marines."

"Can't deny that," Stone said with a smirk, "You and your partner showed up just in the nick of time, that's for sure."

"You wanna make it up to me?" Marshall asked.

"And just how might I do that?" Stone replied with a sly smile.

"I should think ... one beer with a thirsty Marine would do," Marshall replied with a wink.

After pausing a moment, Stone smiled and said, "I think I can do that."

About that time, Stone looked over and saw Cross waving her to the car that had attempted to escape. "Looks like Cross has something," Stone said. "I better go see what he's got."

"Yeah, you better," Marshall replied.

Stone hesitated briefly, then turned and started walking to the car Marshall had shot to pieces when he showed up. "Whatcha got?" Stone asked.

"First off, Marshall is a damn fine shot. He caught this guy twice. Once in the chest and once in the jugular—bled out in seconds. It's not pretty, but get this; I'd bet money that he was the same guy who got away from us the other day when you shot his partner. And, not only that, but this guy has the same features that the girl Chris told us about from *The Spirit of Lake Murray*."

Stone's eyebrows raised, and she asked, "You think he's the one who killed the woman in the emerald dress?"

"I think it's at least possible, and there's only one way to find out for certain. Let's take a headshot of him, then talk to Chris from *The Spirit of Lake Murray* and see if she recognizes him. If so ...."

Stone said, "It's likely that he killed the woman in the emerald dress and was most likely there when Michael Hawkins was killed, too."

"Exactly," Cross replied.

"You know something else?" Stone asked Cross.

"What's that?"

"The boss is going to kill us since we just got our weapons back."

"Could it be possible that he doesn't find out?" Cross asked, hopeful, knowing that was never going to happen.

Before Stone could respond, her phone rang, and after she looked at the screen, she said, "Too late. He knows..."

"How in the hell?" Cross asked.

"He's got ears everywhere," Stone said as she put the call on speaker and answered, "Hey boss."

Stone and Cross heard the disembodied voice of Chief of Detectives Boone shouting, "Can't you two go a single day without firing your weapons? YOU JUST GOT THEM BACK FROM THE LAST TIME!"

"Yes, boss, we know and appreciate everything you did to help us get them back, but this wasn't our fault." Stone replied casually.

"I've already heard what happened from Sergeant Marshall," Boone replied. "Even still, you two will be tied up there the rest of the day. You know that, right?"

"Yes, boss, we know, and before you say it, we know we have a shit-ton of paperwork to do now," Cross said.

Boone sighed and said, "Well, at least you're both okay."

"Yeah, about that," Stone said.

A wave of panic could be heard in Boone's voice as he spouted, "I was told no officers were injured!"

Stone said, "That's true, no officers were, but our cruiser was not so lucky..."

"What ... in ... the ... hell do you mean?" Boone asked through gritted teeth.

"Well, the cruiser took a couple of rounds through the grill. If we're lucky, it's only the radiator, but for now, it's out of action ...we're going to need another ride."

After a long pause, Boone replied, "You two are going to cause me to have a heart attack at forty-eight ... I can see it coming."

Stone said, "Wait, you're only forty-eight? I thought you were older."

"Gee, thanks. I feel like I'm sixty, thanks mainly to you. Once you're done there, get your butts back here and get started on the paperwork."

"Yes, boss," Stone and Cross replied.

ONCE THE SCENE WAS SECURE, Stone, Cross, and the two deputies were taken to the hospital, where they were given a breathalyzer, urine test and had their vitals checked. After being released, they returned to the Sheriff's Department, where they remained for the next several hours doing paperwork on the incident.

At almost eleven o'clock that evening, Stone and Cross left the office after a grueling day. "Want a beer partner?" Cross asked.

Stone thought about it briefly and said, "Nah, I just want my bed. Can you give me a lift home?"

Cross chuckled and said, "No problem, partner. Let's get out of here."

Cross had no sooner pulled out of the department's secure parking lot when he glanced over and saw Stone was already fast asleep. Cross chuckled and said softly, "Good thing I know where I'm going."

After the twenty-minute ride, Cross reached over and gently nudged Stone, saying, "Wake up, partner, we're here."

Stone sat up confused and asked, "Where ... are we?"

"We're at your apartment already. You fell asleep on the way over," Cross said. "You going to be okay getting up to your apartment, or do you want me to walk you up?"

Stone patted Cross on the shoulder and said, "I can take it from here, big guy, but thank you."

"Sure, thang," Cross said as he flashed his patent smile, "but I am going to wait here until I see you walk inside."

"Deal," Stone said as she hopped out and closed the door.

Slowly, Stone walked up the steps to her one-bedroom apartment. When she got to the door, Stone turned and gave Cross a wave, who in turn flashed his lights at her as she unlocked her door and walked in.

Stone closed and locked the door behind her, then reached to turn on the light switch. Before reaching the switch, though, Stone froze, sensing she was not alone in her apartment.

Ever so slowly, Stone instinctively reached for her service weapon and immediately realized that it was not there after it was confiscated yet again after another shooting. Silently cursing the fact that she was again without her service weapon, Stone slowly slid her dominant gun hand around to the small of her back and retrieved the SOG Kiku XR folding knife she kept clipped there.

With a flick of her thumb, the blade folded out effortlessly as Stone thought to herself, *it's better than nothing.*

Turning her back to the wall, Stone took a deep breath and flipped the switch on, anticipating being attacked the instant she turned the light on. Instead, no attack came, and she cautiously looked around to see ... absolutely nothing. Relaxing a moment at not seeing anybody, Stone said aloud, "Damn. I must be wound too tight after today."

Stone took a few deep, calming breaths and dropped her keys in the bowl beside the door. Afterward, she folded her knife and started down the short hallway to her bedroom. As she passed the bathroom, she caught sight of movement out of the corner of her eye at the last second, but it was far too late. The last thing Stone felt was the bite of the probes as the tazer delivered a whopping fifty thousand volts into her side. In less than a second, Stone's body locked up tight.

Before she could recover and on the verge of passing out from from the taser, she was vaguely aware of a figure grabbing her and lowering her to the floor.

13

T he next thing Stone knew, she awoke tied to one of her chairs at the table in her breakfast area. She was not able to see because whoever tied her up had also tied a blindfold over her eyes. She pulled and struggled against the towels that were used to tie her hands to the backs of the chair until she heard a man's voice say, "Relax. You're fine; nobody's going to hurt you."

"That's easy for you to say," Stone barked. "You're not the one blindfolded and tied to a chair. And did you really have to taze me?"

Ignoring the tazer question, the voice said, "Tell ya what, for the moment, I'll take the blindfold off while we talk."

"It's a start," Stone said.

Stone listened intently as the man walked up and started pulling at the knot for the blindfold on the back of Stone's head. After a moment, the blindfold was removed, and Stone could once again see around her living room.

The lights were on, and as she glanced around, she saw only her and her attacker in the room. "Is that better?" the voice asked.

"Marginally," Stone replied as the figure walked around in front of her and squatted down so he was eye-to-eye with her. Looking the man up and down, Stone said, "With that suit ... you have got to be a fed. Who do you work for?"

"It doesn't really matter. Does it?" The man replied without emotion.

"I guess not," Stone said, "What do you want?"

"I need you to understand that you are treading on very thin ice, detective. We know about the Sorrentino syndicate and have an individual on a deep-cover assignment inside the syndicate. It's the first time we have ever gotten anybody anywhere near the Sorrentino family, much less the inner sanctum, and you're about to screw this whole operation up."

"How? All I'm doing is trying to solve a double murder," Stone shot back.

"Yeah, a double murder that is connected directly to the Sorrentino family." The man said.

"How is this connected to a crime family on the West Coast?" Stone asked.

"I can't tell you, but it is." The man replied. You need to leave it alone, detective."

"I'm going to follow the clues wherever they go," Stone asserted.

"Detective ... I can't stress it enough that if this goes south, it will be a career-ender for you," the unidentified man assured Stone.

"It won't go south if you help me a little." Stone said.

"Come now, detective. You know I can't help you," the man said calmly.

Stone countered, saying, "Well, then maybe I can help you."

"What could you possibly have that I need?" The man asked.

Stone didn't want to say but felt she had no choice. She decided to try a bluff, and it worked, "...I have the password."

The unknown man stopped and stared at her for a full minute before saying, "Okay, detective. You now have my attention ... for argument's sake, let's say there is a password that goes to ... something. How did you come by this password?"

"We came across it during our investigation," Stone replied. "The only problem is that we don't know how to use this password. For all we know, it could be anything from an external hard drive to a flash drive or a website. We don't know. Do you?"

After a pause, the man replied, "No, we don't."

"Where do we go from here?" Stone asked.

"We don't go anywhere. This is where we part ways, detective," the man said as he started for the front door.

"Come on, man! You can't leave me here like this," Stone barked.

The man paused momentarily, turned, and said, "Okay, detective, but I'll only untie one hand. You can get yourself free with the other hand while I take the time to disappear. If you're lucky ... we'll never see each other again after this."

"No, if *you're* lucky because the way I see it ... I owe you," Stone said sharply.

"Fair enough," the man said as he untied one of Stone's hands and quickly left her apartment without another word. By the time Stone managed to free herself from the chair and get to the front door, the man was already gone.

The following morning, Stone met Cross in the parking lot. "How was your night?" Stone asked.

"Nice and quiet," Cross replied.

"It was definitely better than mine then," Stone said.

"What do you mean?" Cross asked.

As they walked into the Sheriff's Department and through the bullpen to their shared cubicle, Stone told Cross about the events of her night. Cross apologized, "I am so sorry. I should have walked you up to your door."

Stone patted him on the shoulder and said, "It's ok, big guy. Even if you had, you wouldn't have seen him. I walked right past him and didn't see him until it was too late."

"Yeah, but that doesn't make me feel any better," Cross replied somberly.

"Don't worry about it because we have bigger issues." Stone said.

"Like what?"

"Like the fact that a fed will probably show up here this morning with a federal warrant to take the password and anything else we may have stumbled on, so we are literally running out of time." Stone conceded.

Cross said, "Let's look at it from another way."

"How?"

"All the painting's sent us somewhere else. Right?" Cross asserted.

"Yeah, but not the last one." Stone pointed out.

"That's right, not the last one. I think that means we already have the last piece of the puzzle. We just don't know it." Cross replied.

"It makes sense," Stone said. "Everything was pointing to the password and snippets of the file just to keep us interested."

"Exactly," Cross replied, "What if ...what if we had the answer the entire time?"

"Cross, what are you talking about," Stone asked.

Cross snapped his finger and said, "The only thing we really haven't scanned looking for a hidden QR code is the sketchbook!"

Stone shrugged her shoulders and said, "What have we got to lose? Let's take a look."

Before they had a chance to start looking through the sketchbook, Stone's desk phone started ringing. Stone picked up the phone and said, "Stone here ... yes, boss. Right away." After hanging up the phone, Stone looked at Cross and said, "The boss wants to see us immediately."

"That can't be good," Cross replied.

"Nope, not at all," Stone said as they walked out of their cubicle and headed toward Boone's office.

After the short walk, Stone knocked on Boone's closed door. "Enter," came the muffled reply.

As soon as Stone and Cross stepped inside Boone's office, Stone came face to face with the same man who had tazed her and tied her up the previous night. "WHAT IN THE HELL?" Stone bellowed.

"Good morning, detective. Nice to see you again," the man said.

Cross immediately stepped toward the man and said, "Are you the coward that tazed my partner last night in her own home?"

Stone stuck her arm across Cross's chest and said, "Easy there, big man. Everything's okay," as Cross flexed and released his massive hands.

"CROSS!" Boone snapped, "That's enough. This is Special Agent Sykes with the FBI, and he's here with a warrant for whatever ... evidence you have collected during the case."

"Come on, boss!" Cross snapped.

"Go! And make sure you get all the evidence that has been ... collected." Boone replied as he stared at Stone.

"Yes, boss." Stone said as Special Agent Sykes smirked at her.

"Remember what I said," Stone replied. "Maybe not anytime soon, but I fully plan to wipe that smirk off your face."

"Do be a dear and hurry it up. Would you?" Sykes said, gloating, "I have a case to solve."

"Let's go Cross," Stone said.

"Yeah. Get me out of here before I accidentally fall, and my fist lands on his face." Cross said as he glared at Sykes.

Stone and Cross went downstairs, gathered all the evidence collected during the case, and returned to Boone's office within twenty minutes.

As Stone and Cross re-entered Boone's office holding a large filing box, Sykes stood up and said, "I trust this is everything?"

"Yes. It's everything we have collected during the course of the investigation," Stone replied.

"Very well then. I'll be on my way." Sykes replied as he took the box from Stone, who glared at him.

As Sykes started to leave, Cross suddenly tripped, putting his hands out, and shoved Sykes out the door. Sykes glared over his shoulder at Cross, who simply said, "Whoops."

As Sykes walked out, Boone said, "You two escort him out of this building and get your butts back to my office."

"Yes, boss," both replied.

Stone and Cross followed Sykes all the way to the front door, with

Cross's massive frame trailing Sykes less than a foot from his back. "I assure you I can find my way out of the building," Sykes said.

"I'm sure you can, but you heard our boss just like we did," Cross said almost directly into Sykes' ear.

Cross followed Sykes all the way to the front door and walked outside while Stone hung back slightly, trying not to crack up, laughing at Cross the entire way through the building.

Cross walked to the edge of the parking lot and stood there with his massive arms crossed, watching Sykes as he left. Only when his car pulled out onto the main road did Cross take his eyes off the man's car and start back inside.

As Cross came back inside, Stone said, "You know you scared the shit out of him, don't you?"

"Of course," Cross said with a wink and an evil smile, "that was the intent."

"Come on, let's get back to the boss," Stone said.

After walking quickly back to Boone's office, Stone knocked and opened the door without waiting for permission. "Is he gone?" Boone asked.

"Yep, Cross followed him all the way to the parking lot. If I didn't know any better, I'd say the guy will need to stop somewhere to buy a new pair of underwear because Cross scared him so bad."

Boone shook his head, grinning, and asked, "You did only give him the originals, correct?"

Stone gave Boone a sly smile and said, "Yep, we still have all the copies."

"Excellent, so what are you still standing here for? Get on it!" Boone snapped.

Stone looked at Cross and said, "You heard the man. Let's go check the copies of the sketchbook."

After walking back to their cubicle, Stone and Cross spent the next ten minutes meticulously scanning each hi-res copy of the sketchbook, and on the last page, Cross's phone lit up on yet another hidden QR code.

"There it is!" Cross said excitedly. "Let's see what we have."

Cross hit play, and they heard the same automated voice saying, "LMC."

Cross's eyebrows raised, and he said, "That's it? That's all we get."

Stone smiled and said, "That's all we need. Let's go."

"What do you mean that's all we need? I guess you're driving then if you know where that is."

"Yes, and yes," Stone said as they returned to Boone's office. Stone stuck her head in Boone's door and said, "Hey, boss. We found something. I need a car."

Without saying a word, Boone pointed at Cross standing beside her.

Stone shrugged and said, "I didn't think that would work. Can't blame a girl for trying though. Come on, Cross. It looks like you're driving."

14

Twenty minutes later, Stone and Cross pulled up to the Lexington Medical Center and walked inside. When they walked in, they walked over to the older woman at the information desk, who blushed when she saw Cross's impressive frame walking up.

"Can I help you?" The woman asked as she looked Cross up and down.

"Yes, ma'am, you can," Cross said as he turned on his deep Southern charm. "Can you tell me if the hospital has any artwork hanging up on display, especially from local artists?"

The woman smiled at Cross and said, "Oh, my yes, we have several paintings scattered around the halls, but our newest painting was just donated by a local artist named ... Gabriella Gibson."

Stone said, "Could you please tell us where that painting is?"

"I sure can!" The older woman replied enthusiastically. "Right this way. It's not far at all."

As she got out of her chair, the older woman said, "My name's Betty, and I've been here for twenty years. I must say I've seen many different officers come in here throughout the years, but I have never seen one as ... big as you before."

Cross said, "Thank you, ma'am. I lift a lot of weights and train very hard."

"Yes, I can see you do," Betty said as she wrapped her arm around Cross's massive bicep.

"You know, I also work out quite a bit," Stone said as she tried to get into the conversation.

"Yes, I'm sure you do, deary," Betty replied sarcastically.

After another couple of turns, Betty said, "Here it is. This is our only Gabriella Gibson. Isn't it beautiful?"

"Yes, ma'am, it sure is," Cross replied as he gently unwrapped Betty's arm off his and said, "I'm afraid I need my arm for a minute."

"Oh, silly me," Betty said, blushing as Stone scanned the painting.

"Wait a minute. You won't mess the painting up or take it, will you?" Betty asked.

"No, ma'am," Stone said, as Cross took the painting off the wall so Stone could get to it better.

"Uh huh," Betty said as she glared at Stone.

Betty and Cross walked to a nearby bench, where they took a seat. Betty kept a wary eye on Stone while chatting with Cross, saying, "It's my favorite painting here. I was here at the little ceremony when the artist donated it, ya know."

Cross's eyes widened, and he asked, "You were? This could be very important. Did you see the artist who painted this painting?"

"I sure did. I even managed to snap a quick picture of her even though they asked for no pictures."

Wild-eyed, Cross asked, "Can you show me the picture? Is it on your phone?"

"It sure is," Betty replied proudly.

It took Betty another minute to find the picture, and said, "Here it is."

Cross said, "There are quite a few people in the picture. Can you tell me which one the artist was?"

Betty replied, "I sure can," as she enlarged the photo and pointed to a person—someone neither Stone nor Cross had seen before.

"Can you send me that picture? Cross asked.

"I would be glad to," Betty replied. Moments later, she had airdropped the photo directly to Cross's phone.

While Cross kept Betty occupied, Stone scanned the painting and found something altogether different from an audio file. Once she was done, Stone made eye contact with Cross and gave him a slight nod, indicating she was finished. "Well, Mrs. Betty, my partner and I have everything we need, and I really appreciate this picture. It's going to be a huge help."

"Oh, it's no trouble at all, dear," Betty replied as she patted Cross's massive arm again.

After escorting Betty back to her desk, Cross and Stone quickly exited the hospital. While they walked to his car, Cross asked, "So, did you get it?"

"I got something. It must be a huge file because it took forever to capture," Stone replied.

"Let's play it in the car to ensure the file works and is not corrupt. I don't want to have to come all the way back out here today," Stone said.

"My thoughts exactly," Cross replied.

Stone smiled and said, "It looks like you made a new friend," talking about Betty.

"Looks that way, but she sure didn't care for you much," Cross said, snickering.

"You saw that too?" Stone said, "Old woman was cold as ice to me."

Cross smiled and replied, "Jealous much?"

"Shut up and get in the car," Stone said, laughing.

As the two got into Cross's car, he asked, "I know you were busy with the painting, but did you hear what Betty told me?"

"No, what?" Stone replied.

"They had a little ceremony, and she was there when it was donated. She saw the artist GG."

Stone asked, shocked, "Can she identify her?"

"She can do better than that!" Cross replied, "Even though they were asked not to take pictures, she snapped a quick one when nobody was looking."

"Tell me she sent you a copy!" Stone pleaded.

Cross said, "Please ... with this smile. Who could resist? Of course, I got it."

"Show me, damn it!" Stone said excitedly.

Cross pulled out his phone and said, "The picture was shot from a distance, but there is no doubt..."

"Well, I'll be damned!" Stone replied, shocked, "Who in the hell is that?"

"I have no idea," Cross replied, "but that is definitely not the woman in the emerald dress."

"Nope, it's not," Stone replied, "this woman is in her forties at least."

"This case is starting to get under my skin," Cross snapped.

"Well, maybe this will help," Stone said. "You ready?"

"Of course," Cross replied.

Stone turned the volume up; this time, the QR code directed them to a hidden website asking for a password. Cross looked back in his notes and said, "Try this: WD4OIN. "

After a brief pause, they heard something that would be at the very core of their investigation.

"So, am I to understand that you are offering a partnership?" A male voice asked that sounded like the same voice identified as Mr. Rhodes in an earlier recording.

"No. It's not a partnership. It's more like a business arrangement." The unidentified voice replied with an unusual accent.

"So, you want my people to train your people, and in return ... you will open your supply lines to me so I can move my weapons. Is that what I'm hearing?"

After a brief pause, Stone and Cross heard the unknown male voice reply, *"More or less. Do we have a deal?"*

There was another pause, and then the voice known as Mr. Rhodes could be heard saying, *"My wife is the voice and the CFO of the company. I'll never be able to do this without her consent, and she'll never allow me ..."*

"Allow you to what?... Get into bed with the Sorrentino syndicate? Mr. Rhodes, I happen to know that your business is circling the drain, and you are less than a year away from going broke, which is why you run guns on the side."

"How ... how could you possibly know that?" The voice, identified as Mr. Rhodes, asked.

"I have been watching your company for a while now, and I think working together can mutually benefit both parties." The unknown voice replied.

"Yes, but my wife..."

"Yes, yes ... I know your wife," the unknown voice replied, *"we have already planned for that contingency."*

"What do you mean by that?" Rhodes asked with a worried undertone.

"What I mean is we have arranged a little ... demonstration for you and you alone." The voice said with an evil snicker. *"Bring him in from the other room."*

"Yes, Mr. Sorrentino," a new voice replied.

"WAIT! Did that third voice say, Mr. Sorrentino? As in Sorrentino crime family?" Cross asked.

"Sure did," Stone replied. "If Sorrentino himself was there, the third voice was probably one of his bodyguards."

Stone and Cross listened intently as the sound of a door opening and closing could be heard. Then they heard what could only be described as a scuffle, followed by the sounds of someone being apparently dragged into the room, obviously against their will.

"So, Mr. Rhodes, do you know who this is?" The voice that had been called Mr. Sorrentino asked.

"I ... I know of him, but I do not know him personally," Rhodes replied.

Before anyone else could reply, another voice with a distinctive French accent pleaded, *"What is the meaning of this, Mr. Sorrentino? Whatever you think I've done, I can assure you, you are mistaken..."*

"*Am I?*" Sorrentino replied, "*I have it on good authority that you, my dear Henri ... have been working for the Irish.*"

"*No! It's not true, Monsieur Sorrentino! I swear it! I would never go against our agreement,*" the highly accented voice replied, now in a near panic.

"*Oh no?*" The apparent voice of Sorrentino replied. "*Bring in our esteemed guest.*"

"*What is this? What's going on?*" The voice Stone and Cross now knew as Mr. Rhodes asked.

"What in the hell is this?" Cross asked incredulously as he paused the recording.

"It sounds like somebody, probably this Mr. Rhodes, snuck a recording device into this meeting and got more than he bargained for," Stone replied as she restarted the recording.

Another door could be heard opening and closing, and another very distinct Irish voice could be heard, "*Think you'd get away with it, did ya? Ya see, we smelled your double-cross from a mile away, and well, let's just say ... a little birdie reached out to Mr. Sorrentino and well ... here we all are.*"

"*NO! It is not true, monsieur!* The French voice replied.

"*Oh, but it is,*" Sorrentino replied, "*the entire conversation is recorded...*"

"*Mr. MacGowan, the Sorrentino family extends its gratitude to the MacGowan family for helping to expose this piece of French trash. You may rejoin the party. There is no further need for you to be here.*"

"*Aye, and we look forward to doing business with you in the future,*" The Irish voice replied.

The next thing that could be heard was the sound that every police officer or detective knew—the sound of a pistol being pulled from a leather holster.

"*NO! NO! PLEASE DON'T MONSIEUR SORRENTINO...*"

"*It's too late for you now,*" Sorrentino replied. Two distinct pops followed, followed by the unmistakable sound of a body hitting the floor.

"Holy shit! We just listened to the head of the Sorrentino crime family kill somebody!" Cross replied.

"Yeah, and those two pops were undoubtedly the sound of a suppressed pistol," Stone replied.

"*My God! Why?*" The voice of Rhodes asked.

"*Because, Mr. Rhodes...I wanted you to know what I am capable of.* The supposed voice of the Sorrentino crime family casually replied.

"*Marco,*" Sorrentino said.

"*Yes, boss.*" A new voice replied that appeared to be a bodyguard.

"*Have this mess cleaned up. Take my gun and throw it over the side. If anyone sees you getting rid of my gun ... throw them over the side as well.*"

"*Yes, boss.*" The voice called Marco replied.

After noises of people apparently dragging the body out could be heard, Stone and Cross heard, "Mr. Rhodes, you may rejoin your wife now and see to it that she comes to terms with the arrangement ... or I will. I will expect your answer in two days," Sorrentino replied.

"*Yes, Mr. Sorrentino,*" Rhodes said sheepishly.

Stone and Cross sat there for several moments in stunned silence before Cross said, "Did we just hear the head of the Sorrentino crime syndicate kill someone."

"Sure sounds like it," Stone replied. "Come on, we gotta get back to the Sheriff's department. This is way more than our double murder."

15

Before long, Stone and Cross walked back into the Lexington County Sheriff's Department and straight to Chief of Detective Boone's office. Stone knocked loudly and barged in without waiting for the response, "Chief! We have had a break in the case but we have something you have got to hear!"

Boone looked up from his computer and said, annoyed, "Well, come right in; don't mind the closed door or anything."

"Uh, sorry, but this can't wait," Stone replied.

Boone saw the expressions on Stone and Cross's faces and said, "Okay, what do you have?"

While Stone was getting the recording ready, Cross closed the door and said, "We have something huge, and we're definitely going to need some help on this one."

"Oh, shit ... what have you two found?" Boone asked.

After listening to the entire conversation, Boone took a deep breath and said, "Why ... why do you two always seem to get yourselves into these messes?"

Stone grinned sheepishly and said, "...because we're the best you've got, and we follow the leads wherever they go?"

"Yeah, yeah," Boone replied as he picked up the phone to call *his* bosses, "I'm not even touching this one without help."

Stone and Cross sat and listened while Boone talked to his boss on the phone. When Boone hung up, he said, "Gather all of your information and be prepared to give a detailed account of the case in one hour in the conference room. Be prepared; the brass will be there, so better be sure of everything you say and do."

"Are the feds going to be there?" Cross asked.

"Probably, all I know is my bosses were going to call them," Boone replied.

"We'll be ready, boss," Cross replied as both started to leave his offices to prepare for the meeting.

As they walked, Stone said, "We gotta make sure everything is on point. This could either make us or break us as detectives. This is a once-in-a-lifetime opportunity as far as detectives go."

"Copy that," Cross replied confidently, "it's either heroes or zeros."

"Heroes or zeros," Stone repeated.

ONE HOUR LATER, Stone and Cross walked into the conference room, each with notebooks and folders full of the copied originals under their arms, and closed the door behind them. As soon as they walked in, they saw Chief of Detectives Boone and several other higher-up brass who are usually only seen if there's trouble or a photo to be taken.

"This can't be good," Cross whispered to Stone.

"Let's just present the facts as we know them, and it will be fine," Stone said confidently.

"Oh, I know, it's just that I have never seen so much brass in one room before," Cross replied.

"In a little bit, we'll have them eating out of our hands," Stone said with a wink.

"If I don't piss myself first," Cross whispered with a slight grin.

After everyone got settled in, Chief of Detectives Boone stood up and said, "Okay, now that we're all here, my two best detectives have had a break in a case they have been working on that leads directly back to the Sorrentino crime family in California."

There were mumbles and whispers around the table as Boone continued, "Detectives, the floor is yours. Show everyone what you have found."

Both Stone and Cross stood, and Stone began, "Earlier in the week, Detective Cross and I were dispatched to the scene of an apparent murder. Upon arriving on the scene—"

At that exact moment, the door opened, and a woman in business dress and two men in business suits strode into the room with two pieces of paperwork folded in her hand. The woman announced, "I'm Special Agent Catherine Bozeman of the Federal Bureau of Investigation, and this is a federal warrant for all information concerning the recordings and any information you have regarding the Sorrentino crime family.

In addition, this second piece of paperwork is a gag order forbidding you from talking about the case regarding the Sorrentino family."

Stone snapped, "YOU CAN'T BE SERIOUS?"

"I can, and I am," Bozeman replied sternly. "Did you really think you would get away with that little stunt you tried to pull on Agent Sykes? Who's in charge here?"

The Sheriff, who was also in attendance, stood and said, "I'll take that."

Bozeman snapped, "I want everything, and this time, I mean every single scrap of paper, file, and hair fiber associated with this case. On top of that, I will also be going to each location and taking every single painting directly associated with this case. Is that understood, Sheriff?"

After looking the paperwork over for a few minutes, the Sheriff looked at Special Agent Bozeman and replied, "My Chief of Detectives will see to it that you have everything."

"CHIEF!" Stone snapped.

"DETECTIVE STONE," the Sheriff announced, "there is nothing

we can do. Boone, I expect you to hand over everything personally and don't try to hold anything back."

"Yes, sir," Boone replied.

The Sheriff then announced, "Just so we're clear ... there is a gag order in place, and nobody is allowed to talk about this case anymore once we leave this room. Is that understood?"

People obviously upset about the FBI showing up and taking the case over could be heard mumbling and grumbling, but they could do nothing to stop it. It was a done deal.

Stone jumped up and stormed out of the conference room empty-handed since the feds took her and Cross's notes. "THIS IS ABSO-LUTE BULLSHIT!" Stone yelled as she glared at Special Agent Bozeman.

"Easy there, partner," Cross said. " You don't want to get suspended over this," he continued, guiding her back to their cubicle with his massive arms.

"You can't tell me you're okay with this?" Stone pleaded.

"Of course not, but that's how the game is played with the feds. There has to be something more to what's going on. Otherwise, they would not have come in with guns blazing like they did." Cross replied empathetically.

A few minutes later, Stone plopped in the chair at her desk and sighed. "I see the wheels turning," Cross said. "Whatcha thinking?"

Stone sat in silence, taking a few deep breaths, trying to calm down, then said, "I'm thinking ... I'm thinking I'm gonna call Daven-port. That's what I'm going to do." Stone picked up the phone, but before she could start dialing, she saw movement out of the corner of her eye. Glancing over at the entrance to their cubicle, Stone and Cross saw none other than Special Agent Bozeman standing there.

"I wouldn't do that if I were you," Bozeman said.

"Why, you have some agenda of your own?" Stone snapped.

"No. There's no use in calling Special Agent Davenport because I'm his boss," Bozeman replied calmly.

After a brief pause, Bozeman continued, "Detectives, I just wanted to come by to ensure we had everything and to thank you."

"Yeah, okay, well fu—"

Cross interrupted Stone mid-word, saying, "Uh, what my partner meant to say is, you're welcome, but since we did all the legwork, can you at least give us ... something?"

Bozeman replied empathetically, "Look, I wish I could tell you, but for right now ... I simply can't. There's too much at stake. But I will say this: you can be confident in the fact that you got who was behind the two murders you were investigating. Also, you may want to watch the national news for a while."

As Bozeman turned to leave, Stone said, "Wait! We never found out who the woman in the emerald dress was. Do you know who she is?"

Bozeman paused a moment and then simply said, "Yes." With that, Special Agent Bozeman turned and walked out, never to be seen again.

⁓

AFTER BOZEMAN LEFT, the next few days seemed like a total blur. Neither Stone nor Cross could get the case that had been dubbed 'the woman in the emerald dress' out of their heads, but nothing could be done. Special Agent Bozeman saw to it that everything related to the Sorrentino family was taken with them. She even took Dr. Singh's notes from the coroner's office.

Over the next several days, Stone and Cross made several quiet inquiries but got nowhere. Even her contact in the FBI, namely Davenport, couldn't tell her anything about what had happened.

The only thing they had left of the case were a few names and the name of the yacht *Omertà*. Finally, though, there was a glimmer of hope after several more days. Late one afternoon, while Stone and Cross were sitting in their shared cubicle doing paperwork, the phone on Stone's desk rang.

Cross watched as Stone's eyes lit up while listening to the person on the other end of the phone, and she replied, "We'll be right there."

Stone hung up the phone and said, "Let's go, I'm driving."

"Where are we going?" Cross asked in his thick Alabama accent.

"Tell ya on the way," Stone said.

"That's good enough for me," Cross said as he hopped up and followed Stone out of their cubicle.

A few minutes later, as they were pulling out of the parking lot, Cross looked over at Stone and said, "Okay. You wanna tell me where we're going, or will I have to guess?"

Stone smiled and said, "We're going to see Dr. Singh. He's got something for us."

"On who?" Cross asked, confused.

"The woman in the emerald dress," Stone said, smiling.

"What? How? I thought Bozeman took everything from Singh after she left the Sheriff's Department."

"She did, but Singh had already sent off DNA samples before Bozeman came to see him, and Dr. Singh ... just happened to forget he sent some samples off," Stone said with a sly smile.

"Well, I'll be damned!" Cross replied, "That sneaky old bastard."

Not long afterward, Stone and Cross walked into the coroner's office, and the secretary said, "I'll buzz you in," as soon as she saw them walk in.

Stone and Cross walked through the door at the sound of the buzzing, then walked down the hallway to Singh's office. Stone saw the door was already open, and she stuck her head in, saying, "Hi, Dr. Singh. Please tell me you have something good for us."

"Ah, yes, detectives, please come in and close the door," Singh said.

After Stone and Cross sat opposite him, Singh began, "I wanted to tell you in person the DNA results from the young woman we recently removed from Lake Murray—I believe you refer to her as the woman in the emerald dress."

"Yes, what did you find?" Stone pleaded.

Singh paused and said, "Let me start off by saying, in all my years of performing DNA testing, I have never seen this before."

"Seen what before?" Cross asked.

"Absolutely nothing..." Singh said as his words hit Cross and Stone like a punch in the gut.

"What do you mean?" Cross asked, shocked.

"There are absolutely no hits anywhere on this DNA," Singh answered.

"That ... that's impossible! Isn't it?" Stone said in a statement that there was more disagreement than anything. "I refuse to admit defeat for this woman. There has to be some way we can identify her," Stone pleaded.

Ignoring Stone's pleas, Singh said, "Statistically, the answer is yes. It is impossible that no other person shares DNA with the woman in question. However, the problem lies with the testing. It just means that nobody from her family has had their DNA tested before. Still, the pool of people getting genetic testing for health or historical reasons is growing daily. It is possible that in the future, someone related to her will get some form of genetic testing done, and then ... you could have your answer," Singh said.

"Or it could be something else entirely..." Cross replied as his voice trailed off.

"What are you thinking?" Singh asked.

Cross replied, "What about witness protection?"

Singh paused momentarily and replied, "There is always that possibility. The government can change a person's name and location; however, even the government can't change a person's DNA."

Stone sighed and replied, "Looks like that's it then."

"I'm afraid so, for now anyways," Cross replied.

Both stood, thanked Dr. Singh, and left.

As they left the coroner's office, both were silent, but finally, Cross said, "We're done for the day, so you wanna go grab a beer?"

Stone sighed and replied dejectedly, "I don't feel like it. I think I'm just going home so I can sit on the couch and eat ice cream right out of the tub."

"No problem. I totally understand, "I gotta call Yasmin anyway."

Stone smiled a little for the first time that day and asked, "Have you two decided when you're going out on your first date?"

"Not yet, but when we decide, you'll be the second person to know," Cross replied with a wink.

"Deal," Stone said.

Later that night, Stone did precisely what she said she would do. She was sitting on her couch, wrapped under her favorite thin blanket, eating ice cream and watching television.

Suddenly, the national news cut into the show she was watching and came on with breaking news. As Stone watched, she heard the news reporter state that the FBI was raiding the home of the infamous Lorenzo Sorrentino, one of the biggest crime bosses on the West Coast.

"Holy shit!" Stone said as she grabbed her phone and called Cross. As soon as he answered, Stone shouted excitedly, "TURN ON THE TV!"

"Why, what's going on?" Cross stuttered.

"There's breaking news on right now!" Stone said, unable to contain her excitement, "Sorrentino's getting arrested as we speak!"

Cross quickly turned his television on and said with a smile, "What goes around comes around."

"You watching this?" Stone asked.

"Yep, sure am," Cross replied just as the news broadcaster said Sorrentino was being arrested for the cold-blooded murder of French national Henri Sardou, for starters, among a plethora of other charges.

"Good. Look at who's escorting Sorrentino out!" Stone nearly yelled.

"I see," Cross said, "That's Bozeman...."

"Son of a bitch!" Stone said, "Do you know what that means?"

"Sure do. It means we had a hand in taking down one of the baddest boys on the West Coast." Cross said as he let out a broad grin and watched with growing satisfaction.

"Well, at least we know that ... even if we didn't find out who the woman in the emerald dress was," Stone replied with a bit of disappointment in her voice.

"Someday," Cross replied, "...someday."

Slowly but surely, Stone and Cross got back to normal. They took on new cases and made new arrests but never forgot the woman in the emerald dress. Days turned into weeks, and weeks into a month. Over the course of the next month and a half, Stone, Cross, and, to a lesser extent, Boone followed the downfall of the entire Sorrentino crime syndicate and associates.

In total, seventy-five individuals were arrested, including the entire Sorrentino family and several close associates, including Vincent Marino, one of Sorrentino's top lieutenants, and Frankie Moretti, his lawyer.

In addition to those immediately arrested, the FBI also raided the private security business of Stefan Rhodes, froze all of his assets, and started an investigation into him after the FBI was able to link Sorrentino and Rhodes through an unknown source. With the FBI closing in on him, Stefan Rhodes attempted to flee across the border into Mexico; however, during the high-speed chase, his car ran off the road on a sharp curve and burst into flames, killing him instantly.

With the news of the entire Sorrentino clan behind bars, Stone and Cross resigned themselves to the fact that they may never find out the true story behind the woman in the emerald dress or what part she indeed played in the whole debacle—then everything changed.

TETELESTAI

EPILOGUE

O ne afternoon, while Stone and Cross were sitting at their desk catching up on some much-needed paperwork, the phone on Stone's desk rang. After answering the phone, Cross heard Stone say, "Okay, we will be right there."

"What's up?" Cross asked.

"Somebody at the front desk wants to speak with us," Stone replied.

Cross stood up, gave his shirt a little tug, and said with a smirk, "It's about time the Governor got here with our medals."

"Yeah ... not likely," Stone said with a giggle, "let's go see who it is."

After weaving their way through the bullpen and out to the small waiting area, Stone and Cross saw a woman in her mid-forties with long red hair and an emerald green dress standing there. As the woman turned around to face Stone and Cross, they stopped and stared at her momentarily, each taken aback, obviously thinking the same thing.

After gathering themselves, Stone said, "I'm Detective Stone, and this is my partner Detective Cross. I can't help but feel that we have crossed paths before. Have you ever met me or my partner before?"

"No, but I understand you were looking for me," the attractive woman said somberly.

"I'm sorry, but I don't understand," Cross replied.

"You see, my name is Gabriella Gibson. Do you have somewhere we can talk detective?"

Stone was flabbergasted. So much so, Cross stepped up and said, "Yes, ma'am, right this way," as he, Stone and Gibson went to a nearby conference room.

Now recovered from the shock, Stone said, "Please have a seat, Mrs. Gibson. Please forgive our shock. My partner and I were under the impression that you were dead."

After Gibson, Stone, and Cross took a seat, Gibson replied stoically, "All by design. Now, what can I help you with detectives?"

Stone took a deep breath and said, "Mrs. Gibson, last month, Detective Cross and I worked on two cases that ended up being linked together, and we feel like now that you're here, you can fill in some blanks for us. Can't you?"

Gibson replied somberly, "I think I can ... it doesn't matter now anyway since the Sorrentinos are gone and my husband and daughter are now both dead."

"Did you say, daughter?" Stone asked in disbelief. Before Gibson could answer, Stone continued, "And who was your daughter?"

"You see, my name ... my real name is Cecilia Rhodes," the woman said.

"So if you're Cecilia Rhodes, that means..."

"Quite right, Cecilia replied somberly, "the young woman in the emerald dress who was found in the lake ... was my dear sweet daughter Emily."

Stone looked at Cross and asked, "Wait, why does that name sound so familiar?"

"Because he was the dude that got rolled up with the Sorrentinos," Cross replied, "and he was most likely the same Mr. Rhodes we hear on the tape."

"That's right," Cecilia replied. Stefan Rhodes was my husband."

Stone sat in stunned silence while she processed what she heard.

Finally, she said, "Wait a minute ... if you were somehow mixed up with the Sorrentino crime family on the West Coast, how in the hell did you end up here as a painter?"

"That will require quite a bit of time," Cecilia replied.

"We've got the rest of the day," Stone replied.

"In that case, detectives, could I trouble you for a glass of water or a cup of coffee?"

"Sure thing. Just do me a favor and don't start without me," Cross said with a wink as he stood to get Cecilia a cup of coffee. "I want to hear every word of this."

After Cross walked out, Stone noticed a single tear sliding down Cecilia's face and asked, "Are you all right?"

Wiping away the tear, Cecilia replied, "As okay as one could be expected after losing everything."

The door opened, and Cross came back in with a cup of coffee for Cecilia and several packets of sugar and powdered creamer, "Sorry, but this is all we have," Cross replied.

After she fixed her coffee, Cecilia said, "For clarification, the downfall started several years prior with several bad business decisions on my ex-husband's part. We, of course, didn't know it at the time, but the Sorrentino crime syndicate had been watching my husband's private security business with quite a bit of interest, apparently.

Stone said, "Let me guess, Sorrentino approached you with a promise of saving the business if you worked with him? Was it something like that?"

"More or less," Cecilia replied. "Sorrentino had approached my husband and me several times, making offers to help the business. Stefan wanted to, but I, being the CFO and face of the company, said no."

"What happened?" Cross asked.

"Suddenly, we were invited to a dinner cruise onboard a yacht called the *Omertà*. I didn't know it at the time, but my husband must have known something was going to happen, so he decided to wear a recording device the night of the dinner disguised as an insulin pump."

"So, your husband tried to get a little insurance on Sorrentino but got more than he bargained for," Stone stated.

"Exactly. Anyway, the night of the party, Stefan was summoned into a room that was off-limits to the other guests. When he returned, he was white as a ghost and refused to talk about what he had seen or heard. Instead, he slipped the disguised recorder off and told me to put it in my purse for safekeeping, and that's how I ended up in the middle of an undercover operation," Cecilia said sadly.

"I don't understand," Stone said.

"Stefan and I had an argument at the table afterward, so I grabbed my purse and went out on deck to be alone. I saw a beast of a man tossing something down to a small black boat that had pulled alongside the yacht. The man saw me, and before I knew what happened, he told me to either get in the boat or he was going to kill me, so I did. As it turns out, he wasn't going to kill me. That was a ploy to get me to leave and get on the boat. It was an FBI boat, and that man was an undercover FBI agent posing as Sorrentino's bodyguard."

"Holy ... shit," Cross muttered.

"And that explains why neither Davenport nor Bozeman could say anything about it," Stone replied.

Cecilia sat somberly and said, "From then on ... I've been a ghost. After being snatched off the boat, it was made to look like I fell overboard and drowned. After that, the FBI told me I had to disappear. I felt I couldn't trust anybody, so I never told them about the recording device."

"And they didn't find the recorder?" Cross asked.

"They saw it, but they never questioned it because I put the insulin pump on like it was mine," Cecilia replied, "as soon as I was relocated here and able, I transferred the recording to a flash drive."

"So, how did your daughter get involved in everything?" Stone asked.

"As it turns out, my daughter had already applied and received a full-ride scholarship with the university here, which is why I think they relocated me here," Cecilia said, thinking of the first time she saw her daughter after her death was reported.

"That must have been a hell of a shock," Stone replied.

"Oh, indeed it was. Now that we were together again, we were determined never to lose each other. As you can imagine, our trust in the system was seriously in doubt by then, so I devised a little insurance policy."

"The QR codes in the paintings," Stone realized.

"Exactly," Cecilia replied, "the only thing was I never expected people to want my painting. Nobody ever showed them any interest in California, but people were begging for them here. So, I invented the name Gabriella Gibson and tried to stay out of the public eye. To my astonishment, I was found by a man named Michael Hawkins, who was an art broker, about selling my paintings."

"And that's how we got pulled into it," Cross replied. "We were tasked with investigating his death."

"Another innocent person ... dead because of what happened," Cecilia said with a crack in her voice. "He was a good man. He was the only person on this coast who knew our story," Cecilia said sadly as she sipped her coffee.

"So ... how did your daughter end up on *The Spirit of Lake Murray* that night?" Stone asked cautiously.

Cecilia paused and smiled, obviously thinking about her daughter, then said, "We were always careful. Whenever Michael needed to meet, Emily went instead, acting as a buffer or go-between. Somehow, and I have no idea how, but somehow, Sorrentino's goons found Michael Hawkins. My daughter was supposed to meet him on *The Spirit of Lake Murray* that night to review plans for a new painting dedication."

"It makes sense now," Stone said, looking at Cross, "Sorrentino's boys found Hawkins, got him to talk, and arranged to have someone..." Stone stopped, choosing not to say anymore to spare Cecilia from hearing the rest.

Cecilia simply nodded and said, "Someone must have killed her that night thinking she was me because we both love emerald colors and had multiple emerald dresses." Then Cecilia burst into tears. After recovering sufficiently, Cecilia wiped her tears, stood, and said, "Well, I've taken enough of your time. Thank you, detectives, for everything you have done."

"You are most welcome, Cross replied somberly.

"What will you do now? Where will you go?" Stone asked.

"I have no idea. I have nothing at all," Cecilia said as she fought back tears, "who could have known..."

"Known what?" Stone asked as Cecilia's lip quivered, trying to keep from crying yet again.

"That one small decision, like choosing to take that damned recorder that night, would have caused all this chaos and turmoil."

"Well, it's over now, and you do have your paintings," Cross said, trying to cheer her up and help Cecilia see at least a glimmer of hope.

"I suppose," Cecilia replied softly before turning and walking out.

After Cecilia left the conference room, Stone said, "Damn, my heart breaks for her. She and her daughter got pulled into a mess neither one of them wanted to be in."

"Yeah, it's tragic. Hopefully, she can find peace one day," Cross replied somberly.

LATER THAT EVENING, as the sun went down, the Lexington County Sheriff's Department received a call to go to the Irmo side of the Lake Murray Dam. A woman in a dark green dress had been seen standing on the dock at the Recreation Area crying, and the caller was worried about her safety.

Several deputies were dispatched to the area, but nothing was found. Two days later, Stone and Cross were again called to the scene of another body recovery near the famous towers of Lake Murray. Both Stone and Cross were shocked and saddened to see that the body was none other than—Cecilia Rhodes. The Sorrentino syndicate had taken its last victim.

ABOUT THE AUTHOR

Steven Jacobs, a native of Wilmington, North Carolina, was captivated by history from a young age. His fascination was nurtured by his father, who introduced him to classic movies featuring legendary actors like Cary Grant, John Wayne, Henry Fonda, and Steve McQueen. This early exposure sparked Steven's passion for history, particularly the turbulent years of the early to mid-1900s, and his love for military history began to bloom.

Later in high school, Steven excelled in United States history, especially in the turbulent years of the early to mid-1900s, and this is where his love for military history flourished. By the time Steven was thirty-five years old, he had read countless books on United States history with a focus on the era of World War II.

At the age of forty-five, Steven penned his debut book, The Disappearance of U-491, a gripping tale about a German U-boat vanishing during World War II. The experience of writing this book was so fulfilling that he decided to continue, culminating in the completion of his fourteenth book. This impressive body of work is a testament to his dedication and love for historical fiction.

Now, at the age of fifty-three, Steven lives in Columbia, South Carolina. He has worked for the government for fifteen years.

Please 'like' and follow his Author's Facebook page for updates and sneak peeks at other books in the works. Also, feel free to write a review on Amazon, Barnes and Noble, and anywhere else these books are sold.

www.ingramcontent.com/pod-product-compliance
Lightning Source LLC
Chambersburg PA
CBHW050451110726
47899CB00003B/900